D1527074

GAFFE OUT LOUD

THE WORST DETECTIVE EVER, BOOK 7

CHRISTY BARRITT

River Heights

COMPLETE BOOK LIST

Squeaky Clean Mysteries:

   #1 Hazardous Duty

   #2 Suspicious Minds

   #2.5 It Came Upon a Midnight Crime (novella)

   #3 Organized Grime

   #4 Dirty Deeds

   #5 The Scum of All Fears

   #6 To Love, Honor and Perish

   #7 Mucky Streak

   #8 Foul Play

   #9 Broom & Gloom

   #10 Dust and Obey

   #11 Thrill Squeaker

   #11.5 Swept Away (novella)

   #12 Cunning Attractions

   #13 Cold Case: Clean Getaway

#14 Cold Case: Clean Sweep

#15 Cold Case: Clean Break

#16 Cleans to an End

While You Were Sweeping, A Riley Thomas Spinoff

The Sierra Files:

#1 Pounced

#2 Hunted

#3 Pranced

#4 Rattled

The Gabby St. Claire Diaries (a Tween Mystery series):

#1 The Curtain Call Caper

#2 The Disappearing Dog Dilemma

#3 The Bungled Bike Burglaries

The Worst Detective Ever

#1 Ready to Fumble

#2 Reign of Error

#3 Safety in Blunders

#4 Join the Flub

#5 Blooper Freak

#6 Flaw Abiding Citizen

#7 Gaffe Out Loud

#8 Joke and Dagger

#9 Wreck the Halls

#5 Bound by Mayhem

Vanishing Ranch

#1 Forgotten Secrets

#2 Necessary Risk

#3 Risky Ambition

#4 Deadly Intent

#5 Lethal Betrayal

#6 High Stakes Deception

#7 Fatal Vendetta

#8 Troubled Tidings

#9 Narrow Escape

The Sidekick's Survival Guide

#1 The Art of Eavesdropping

#2 The Perks of Meddling

#3 The Exercise of Interfering

#4 The Practice of Prying

#5 The Skill of Snooping

#6 The Craft of Being Covert

Saltwater Cowboys

#1 Saltwater Cowboy

#2 Breakwater Protector

#3 Cape Corral Keeper

#4 Seagrass Secrets

#5 Driftwood Danger

#6 Unwavering Security

Beach House Mysteries

    #1 The Cottage on Ghost Lane

    #2 The Inn on Hanging Hill

    #3 The House on Dagger Point

School of Hard Rocks Mysteries

    #1 The Treble with Murder

    #2 Crime Strikes a Chord

    #3 Tone Death

Carolina Moon Series

    #1 Home Before Dark

    #2 Gone By Dark

    #3 Wait Until Dark

    #4 Light the Dark

    #5 Taken By Dark

Suburban Sleuth Mysteries:

    Death of the Couch Potato's Wife

Fog Lake Suspense:

    #1 Edge of Peril

    #2 Margin of Error

    #3 Brink of Danger

    #4 Line of Duty

    #5 Legacy of Lies

    #6 Secrets of Shame

    #7 Refuge of Redemption

Cape Thomas Series:

#1 Dubiosity

#2 Disillusioned

#3 Distorted

Standalone Romantic Mystery:

The Good Girl

Suspense:

Imperfect

The Wrecking

Sweet Christmas Novella:

Home to Chestnut Grove

Standalone Romantic-Suspense:

Keeping Guard

The Last Target

Race Against Time

Ricochet

Key Witness

Lifeline

High-Stakes Holiday Reunion

Desperate Measures

Hidden Agenda

Mountain Hideaway

Dark Harbor

Shadow of Suspicion

The Baby Assignment

The Cradle Conspiracy

Trained to Defend

Mountain Survival

Dangerous Mountain Rescue

Nonfiction:

Characters in the Kitchen

Changed: True Stories of Finding God through Christian Music (out of print)

The Novel in Me: The Beginner's Guide to Writing and Publishing a Novel (out of print)

CHAPTER
ONE

"OH. My. Goodness. There aren't his and her sinks in this ensuite?" I paused dramatically, making sure my eyes were wide with disbelief as I stood in the center of the master bathroom.

Jackson Sullivan ran a finger along the golden-colored granite, totally unaffected by my dramatics. "Well, you are the only one living here, Joey."

"But this bathroom surround is made out of molded plastic. *Molded plastic.* And it's beige. Who does that anymore?"

Jackson shrugged, amusement dancing in his eyes. "A lot of builders in this area. Molded plastic is very cost-effective."

I let out a sigh, realizing I wasn't getting my point through to him. The man might be handsome with his fit build, killer blue eyes, and scruffy facial hair, but when it came to soap opera worthy melodramatics, he had no clue. He was all logical, like he should be a detective or something.

Maybe that was good since he *was* a detective. But nonetheless.

I needed him to feed my dramatic energy right now. "But there are no stainless-steel appliances in the kitchen and the countertops are granite, and I want marble. And what about an open floor plan? Do these people not know how important that is to today's homeowners? How can I see my kids while I'm cooking in the kitchen with that big wall up?"

Jackson crossed his muscular arms across his equally muscular chest and gave an even-keel stare. "You don't have any kids. And you don't cook."

"I don't know what else to say." I raised a shoulder and let out a snobby sigh. "But this place isn't up to today's standards."

"It *was* built a hundred years ago."

"Since I just bought the place, I guess I'll get used to it."

As Jackson cracked a smile, I broke character. As much fun as it had been pretending to be an uptight buyer from a reality TV show, I really didn't care about any of those things I'd just mentioned. I loved this place.

The 3,000-square-foot "cottage" was my new home here in Nags Head, North Carolina. Everything about this place was far, far away from my old life in LA—and that was a good thing. A very good thing.

In fact, when I stepped through one of many sets of sliding glass doors that ran along the entire living room wall, the Atlantic Ocean greeted me, along with a wraparound deck and a lifetime of opportunities to make my hopeful future different from my anguished past. I considered this Step 278 in disaster cleanup efforts.

"What disaster?" you might ask.

My life.

But the best part about buying this home was the fact that Jackson Sullivan lived nearby. And anywhere I could be with Jackson was a good place.

I wandered back into the kitchen and pulled myself up until I perched on the kitchen counter. Something crinkled in my back pocket, and I reached for the mystery object.

Objects.

Actually, photos.

"I'm glad I found these as I was packing this morning." I handed them to Jackson. "I've been meaning to give them to you."

He glanced through them, studying each one curiously. There was one of me on the beach with the sun hitting my hair at just the right angle. Another was a studio shot where I wasn't smiling, but my eyes clearly stated intelligence. In the third, I laughed after someone told me a joke. My body was bent forward as the laugh captured me entirely.

Jackson kept his head lowered, only raising his gaze. "These are great pictures, but what are they for? To put on my nightstand?"

"No, these are for you to have on hand in case of an emergency."

"What kind of emergency would I need these for?"

"You know, if I ever disappear. These are the pictures I want you to give to the media."

A wrinkle formed between Jackson's eyebrows. "You know this isn't a normal conversation, right?"

I shrugged. "I know, but I'm just saying. Some of the pictures that relatives use of their loved ones during moments of crisis are so unflattering."

A deep, rumbling chuckle finally emerged from Jackson. He looked away and shook his head, almost as if he didn't quite know what to do with me. Considering the fact that he'd known me for six months now, I'd say that was a good thing. I liked to keep people guessing.

It made life more interesting.

"You're a piece of work." Jackson ran a hand over his face. "You know that, don't you, Joey Darling?"

I shrugged one shoulder and pursed my lips. "Why, yes I do. You're welcome."

"You're welcome?"

"Because you'll never have a dull moment with me around."

Jackson stepped closer, his eyes dancing with mischief. "No, I won't."

He planted a hand on each side of me, effectively trapping me where I sat there on the kitchen counter.

I was okay with that.

Mostly because I was okay with Jackson. More than okay, for that matter.

I loved him. And I hadn't been sure I would ever love anyone again after my last relationship fiasco.

I looped my arms around his neck, like I'd done a million times before. He leaned close, his lips meeting mine. Also like they'd done a million times before.

But, as his lips lingered on mine, a knock sounded at the door. Jackson hung his head with frustration and sighed. We'd had lots of interruptions lately, and alone time had been hard to come by.

Jackson stepped back. "We can finish that later."

"I'll think about it." Yes, something about the man brought out my sass.

It beat what my ex-husband had brought out in me. Insecurity and fear.

The two men were like night and day.

"I guess I should answer that." I didn't move.

Jackson didn't budge either. "I guess you should."

"Or we could ignore it . . ."

"Joey, are you there?" a deep voice called. "I see your car outside."

I recognized that voice. Zane Oakley.

My friend had returned from his trip to Florida two weeks ago, and he'd been my realtor for this deal. He'd said he would stop by my new house to pick up something the previous owner had mistakenly left in one of the upstairs bedrooms.

As I opened the door, Zane thrust some flowers into my hands. "Congrats! You're now the proud new owner of one of the best properties on the Outer Banks."

"I know. I am, aren't I? I can't believe it." I really couldn't. I mean, I'd owned a house before. But then I'd lost my marriage, my career, and my money. I wasn't sure I'd ever regain those things again.

And I was okay with it. There were more important things in life than money and career.

And my marriage . . . well, no marriage should be like mine had turned out. I'd had more bruises and cuts than I'd had love and kisses. I'd had more insults than words of affirmation. And I'd had more nights where I'd fallen asleep crying than I'd had nights I'd gone to sleep in my loved one's arms.

But still, buying this house was a big step. I'd moved across the country, far away from the vortex I called Hollywood. Getting away was one of the best things I could have done. Had I mentioned that yet?

Zane, with his curly hair, board shorts, and plain tee looked like the epitome of a beachside real estate agent as he stood in front of me, especially since he wore loafers instead of flip-flops. That alone distinguished professional Zane from surfer Zane.

"Hello, Jackson." Zane nodded at Jackson, looking stiffer than a corpse during a confrontation.

Jackson nodded back, just as corpse-like. "Zane."

Oh, no. I didn't want to go there now. The two men had kept a rivalry going for too long. I'd clearly chosen Jackson, so there was no need for it to continue.

Instead, I clapped my hands. "So, what did you need to pick up, Zane?"

"I guess Wesley left a painting under a bed upstairs. He called and asked if I would mail it to him. I was supposed to check this morning but forgot."

Wesley Twigg had owned this house for the past five years. He was an artist—a painter—who'd found inspiration from the water. However, though the man was only in his fifties, he'd recently been diagnosed with a heart condition. Because of that, he'd sold the house and moved up north to be closer to his cardiac specialist.

He'd moved out a week ago and had done the closing remotely, so I hadn't actually met him.

"I want to see this mysterious painting," I said.

"Maybe it's worth a lot of money. Possession is nine-tenths of the law."

"Actually, that's a fallacy when you have proper evidence that proves . . . never mind." Jackson shook his head.

I had no idea what kind of stuff this Wesley guy painted, but I assumed it was landscapes of the beach. I assumed if he could afford this house, he was pretty successful. The only reason I could afford it was because my last movie, *Family Secrets*, had done exceedingly well.

"Then follow me."

We walked through the wood-paneled living room. Only, this wood paneling had been painted a pale gray color.

Then we walked through the kitchen with its white cabinets and gray granite countertop that reminded me of a meteorite that had been repurposed.

Take that, HGTV.

A master bedroom was tucked into a corner on the first floor, and four bedrooms were upstairs. On a lower story there was a game room and laundry.

Oh, that wasn't to mention the balconies. The many, many balconies and decks that displayed the ocean just on the other side of the dune.

There had been no way I could pass up this property.

Wesley had left most of his furniture here, but none of it was my style. I'd be buying my own soon, and probably with the help of a decorator. But, until then, at least I had something I could use, even if the dark brown leather couches reminded me of something you'd find at a shrink's office.

We climbed the stairs to the top floor, and Zane opened the door to the final bedroom down the hallway. I stepped inside, fully expecting it to be fine just like everything else in the house was.

But as I pranced toward the window to fix a wayward curtain, I paused and sucked in a breath.

A woman lay on the floor beside the bed, just out of sight from the doorway.

"Joey?" Jackson paused as he stepped inside the room.

I didn't even have any words. No, I just pointed and gaped. Was she . . . dead?

And then I realized the truth, and I laughed. I laughed out loud, and I laughed hard.

Relief flushed through me, and I chided myself for being so gullible.

I turned to Jackson, who remained straight-faced. He was a better actor than I'd thought. "Who put you up to this?"

"Put me up to what?" Jackson's eyebrows inched together as he stepped around me. His eyes widened when he saw what I saw. He almost looked genuinely surprised as he knelt there, examining the "woman." Hollywood had amazing effects that could make even fake people look real.

"It was Mark Johnson, wasn't it?" I shook my head. This one was good. Really good. Maybe his best.

"Who's Mark Johnson?" Jackson turned the woman over, and her silky brown hair fell over her face.

There was no blood to be seen.

Of *course*.

Because this wasn't a real body.

This was a joke.

"You're a better actor than I thought. As I'm sure you know, Mark Johnson is one of the producers for *Relentless.*" *Relentless* was the TV show I starred in as an ace detective. It had just been picked up by Netflix and would start filming new episodes in one week. "Every time someone on one of his shows buys a new home, he pranks them. He must have gotten someone to leave this dummy here. Good one."

I'd fallen for it. Totally fallen for it. Then again, given my track record . . .

Jackson remained on the floor, kneeling by the body, and his eyes met mine. "Joey, this isn't a dummy."

I stared at him, waiting for him to crack a smile and say that the joke was on me. Mark must have been convincing if he talked straight-laced Jackson into participating in this little charade.

But Jackson didn't smile.

I shifted, not quite wanting to believe what I thought I should probably start believing. "What do you mean?"

Was there some kind of dummy joke coming on here? Maybe it started with, "Why did the dummy cross the road?" Or maybe there was a judgment coming. Had calling a dummy a dummy suddenly become non-PC? I couldn't keep up.

Jackson grimaced. "I mean, this is a real woman. And she's dead. In your new home."

CHAPTER
TWO

I WAVED my hand in front of my face trying to cool my skin, which was hot with emotion, as I paced the deck of my new place. My new place that had been tarnished with a dead body.

Why me? Why did these things always happen to me?

I didn't want to be one of those people who thought the world was out to get them. I really didn't. But couldn't I just have one thing in my life go smoothly? Just one thing?

What did this mean for my house? Could I give it back? Unsign all those closing papers? A tiny little apartment away from all this was sounding better and better. Someone could have even died in it. As long as I didn't know about it, I'd be fine.

"How are you doing?" Zane joined me by the railing.

He was a good friend. A good listener. And as long as he remembered that we were just friends, we'd be okay. And as long as he kept the demons from his past in his past.

Drug use was like the tide. Sometimes it ebbed farther out than it had before and the waves were peaceful and calm. But the pull of the water was always there, waiting to erode the shoreline when you weren't on guard.

I stared out at the ocean, which was a beautiful green-blue today. Tourists in bathing suits played all along the shore and in the water, enjoying their vacation.

They were totally clueless as to what was happening just over this dune in the beautiful, old non-HGTV-worthy beach house.

"I'm doing about as well as you can imagine." I shivered, even though it wasn't cold outside. No, it was uncomfortably hot and as steamy as a naughty romance novel. "Can I undo all of this?"

He frowned. "Sorry. If this had happened a day earlier, we'd be golden. The deal would be off. But . . ."

"Yeah, I know." I drew my hands closer, missing those days when I had someone to take care of me. When my dad would tell me everything would be okay. Basically, I missed the days when I didn't have to adult. Why had I ever been in such a hurry to grow up?

"You can stay at my place."

I snorted and waited for him to laugh. He didn't. "Thanks for the offer, but I don't think that's a good idea."

"You need a massage?" He wiggled his fingers—but still didn't laugh. "Hashtag: available."

"Also not a good idea." Zane was also a massage therapist, so . . . yeah. But no. I sighed. "What do you think happened to that woman, Zane?"

He twisted his lips as he turned his gaze toward the beach. "I have no idea. There wasn't any blood."

"Rigor mortis had set in. Her limbs were so stiff that I thought . . ." I couldn't finish. But I'd thought the woman was a wax figure or something equally as fake. That was the truth of the matter.

I mean, who finds a dead body in her house before the ink on the closing papers could even dry?

Me, that's who.

Zane squeezed my shoulder. "I know, Joey. I know. This really stinks."

I leaned on my elbows against the railing, suddenly finding it hard to stand. "What am I going to do?"

"You'll think of something. You always bounce

back, no matter what happens. You're like the Come-back Kid."

I hardly heard him. How would I ever get over knowing someone had died here? I didn't know if I could. "There's no way I can stay here and not remember finding that body."

"It doesn't look like this was the scene of the crime, if that makes it any better. I mean, there were no signs of struggle." He shifted. "What can I do for you?"

I straightened, realizing I had to pull myself together right now. "There's nothing you can do. But thanks."

He glanced at his watch and sighed. "Listen, I hate to do this to you, but I've got another showing to do. I really need a few more sales under my belt if I'm going to get back on track. Do you mind?"

"No, go right ahead. I'm hoping Jackson and his crime-fighting posse will be done soon." Also known as Jackson and two other NHPD officers. "Sorry you couldn't get the painting."

"Maybe once the scene is cleared. Anyway, call me if you need me."

"Of course."

No sooner had Zane left than another car pulled up to the scene. I recognized the vehicle right away, but I had no idea why the occupants were here. A moment later, my aunt Dizzy and her friends Geraldine, Maxine, and MaryAnn all scrambled out with balloons and flowers in their hands.

The group called themselves the Hot Chicks. Dizzy was my aunt by marriage, a hair "dresser," and a hoot. She and her friends never failed to amuse me.

That said, I braced myself because I knew what was coming.

They scrambled up the steps—as fast as their aging bodies would allow—and greeted me with wide, excited smiles, as if I'd won an Oscar and three police cars now had to escort me everywhere.

I mean, really . . . had they not seen the police cars out front?

"Congratulations, Joey!" Dizzy's big smile might scare young children, especially when coupled with her cartoon-like blue eye shadow. But her heart was good. "We're just so happy for you! We wanted to give you a little housewarming surprise."

"Now we'll get to see you all the time since you're staying in the area," Maxine said. "And you can pick out anything free from my store—as long as it's under twenty-five dollars."

She owned a fabulous store called Utter Clutter that sold repurposed decorations. Twenty-five dollars there would get me a couple of new drawer pulls. Too bad I'd probably need twenty.

"That was our prayer—that you would stay in the

Outer Banks," MaryAnn added. She was the quiet, sweet one of the group, the person I gravitated toward when I needed normalcy.

I raised my hands in a *ta-da!* fashion, just deciding to humor them a moment. "And here I am! Answered prayers, right?"

"Can we see the place?" Dizzy glanced beyond me at the house.

"Not right now." I followed her gaze to the window, where I spotted two officers still inside the house. "It's a bad time."

Dizzy's smile disappeared. "Are you having a party you didn't invite us to?"

"What? Why would you think that?" Confusion nipped at me.

"It's plain to see that Jackson's friends are here." More hurt lined Dizzy's voice.

I couldn't help but laugh just a little as I realized why she'd misunderstood. "That's why you think all the police cars are here?"

"Adding insult to injury by laughing at our rejection? Have you already forgotten the small people in your life?" Geraldine drew her head back in offense. "I didn't think you were the type, Joey Darling."

I shook my head quickly, knowing I needed to set them straight before this went any further. "No, no. I'm sorry. This is . . . I don't even know how to say this. It's not funny at all."

"We don't think so either." MaryAnn frowned, looking like I'd just told her we couldn't be friends anymore.

"Ladies, the police aren't here because I'm having a party. The police are here because I found a dead body inside."

They all gasped, almost like they'd practiced the act together in a theater class. I was impressed by their non-coordinated coordination.

"A. Dead. Body?" Dizzy's eyes were as wide as my hips had been in that movie after the camera added ten pounds.

"I know. It sounds crazy, doesn't it?" I still couldn't believe it. Any of my earlier humor disappeared—coincidentally, that was also like my hips, only this time after I'd seen them on the big screen. That had been the start of my string of crash diets. Seeing yourself onscreen could bring out the worst insecurities.

"I'm so sorry, Joey," MaryAnn said. "Now you have to live with a ghost."

"Ghosts aren't real," I said, trying to remind myself as well. "Besides, we don't know that this woman died here. She . . . well, we don't know yet."

"I guess you'll be finding out soon enough." Dizzy made a ghostly sound and widened her eyes in mock horror.

I frowned. I guess I would be.

The Hot Chicks left five minutes later. I'd had to shoo them away because they were getting a little too curious and trying to peer in the windows. They'd left just in the nick of time because Jackson stepped out onto the deck. Of course his eagle-eyed gaze went right to Dizzy's car as she backed from the driveway.

"Dizzy was here?" He still stared at her car as stray beams of sunlight filtered from between the slats of the deck above us and hit his handsome features.

"Yep. Came to see the house. With all her friends." The breeze, thick with humidity, hit me just then. I had to admit that I wasn't crazy about the humidity. Especially since it was July. The air just felt like Jell-O. Hot Jell-O.

Jackson turned back to me, his eyelids lowered with dread. "Please tell me you didn't mention the body."

My stomach clenched as I mentally reviewed exactly what I'd said. "What do you mean?"

I had to buy myself some time.

"I mean, we decided not to leak this news yet. We want to keep it quiet until we can find out more details about who this woman is and how she died."

I could explain this. It wasn't like I'd called them

over and announced the news. "Well . . . the Hot Chicks thought I was having a party with your police officer friends and that I hadn't invited them. I had to set them straight. I mean, you should have seen the rejected look in their eyes. I felt like I was Kristen Bell leaving Jason Segel on the side of the road in *Forgetting Sarah Marshall*.

Jackson leveled his gaze, unaffected by my histrionics. "So you told them?"

"I had no choice."

"This will be all over town in thirty minutes or less."

"I didn't know. I'm sorry." Just when I'd thought I was doing better learning the realities of police investigations . . . I learned that I wasn't. Beauty wasn't the only unreachable standard Hollywood set for the masses.

Yay for me.

"It's okay, Joey." Jackson touched my wrist.

"A dead body was found in my house. It doesn't really feel okay."

He pulled me into his embrace, and I melted there. Nothing felt better than feeling those muscular arms around me and smelling his spicy aftershave.

"I know it doesn't. I know." His voice had a soothing tone that I'd only ever heard him use with me. And I liked that. I liked feeling I brought out a softer side of him. Someone needed to.

"I'm at a loss, Jackson. I mean, I don't even know what to do. I was going to go shopping for some furniture. And we're supposed to go out to eat and celebrate—"

He nudged me closer. "We can still go out to eat. Just later. Tonight."

I nodded. "Okay."

"But, unfortunately, I have to work this case right now. I wish I could stay with you. I really do, but . . ."

"I know. This is part of your job." I couldn't even hide my disappointment. I didn't want to face the next few hours alone. No, I wanted to pretend like none of this had ever happened and continue on my merry way.

Jackson pulled away until our gazes connected. He rested his hand on my neck, his fingers gently intertwining with my hair. "Why don't you see if Phoebe is available? Do you want me to call her for you?"

"No, I can do it. Or maybe I'll go inside and look for some garlic."

"What?"

I shrugged. "To ward off the spirits."

"You mean vampires? Garlic is for vampires."

"Potato, potato."

"Unfortunately, you can't go back inside now. The crime scene guys are still working the place."

My beautiful, unblemished home was now going

to be blemished with fingerprint dust and crime-scene tape. Maybe a body outline? Sometimes they even had to take out pieces of walls or floors or rugs.

Yet I hadn't seen blood, so . . . "How did she die, Jackson?"

He pressed his lips together and tilted his head. "You know I can't tell you that."

"Who is she?"

"Nope, couldn't tell you that either—if we knew. I can see that look in your eyes. That drive to find answers. But just let me handle this, okay? You have only one more week here before you leave for filming. Just enjoy yourself. Work on memorizing your script. Don't concern yourself with this investigation."

I nodded, even though I didn't want to. Concerning myself with investigations had become my schtick. It was what I did.

Instead, I said, "Okay."

But this would be like a chronic dieter staring at a piece of chocolate cake and trying not to eat it. I was that dieter, and I usually ended up eating the cake.

He kissed my forehead, seeming appeased by my answer. "I'll call you in a few hours, okay? Dinner is still on."

"Dinner's still on . . ."

I should be excited. And I was. Jackson could easily blow off our date, and he wasn't doing that. It was just that . . . after everything that happened . . . I had no idea what to do with myself right now.

Again, I pulled myself together—because that's what strong, capable women did. "I'll see you tonight."

Jackson paused before heading back inside and studied my expression for a split second. "Just to clarify, this has nothing to do with you, right? You've never seen that woman."

"Of course I haven't. Why would you ask?"

"Because you have a knack for being connected with some of the crimes in this area. I just wanted to check."

"I've definitely never seen the woman before. Maybe she's connected with the previous owner. But not me."

Nope, not me. And, as Jackson had reminded me, I was leaving in one week. I had a script to memorize. Five pounds to lose. The start of a zit that I needed to zap.

There was no way I was getting involved with this investigation.

Not this time.

The only problem was that I couldn't be sure I'd be able to sleep in my own house until this crime was solved. And no sleep wouldn't bode well for my on-camera comeback.

CHAPTER
THREE

AFTER JACKSON HAD DEPARTED, I remained outside, unsure what to do with myself now that my house was a crime scene. So I sat there —on the deck boards since there was no furniture— with my back against the cedar siding. At least it was covered and shaded. Despite that, sweat still trickled down my back.

Two officers remained, wrapping things up. The medical examiner had carried the body away. People on the beach and then on the sidewalk had stopped to stare, most likely wondering what bad thing could have possibly happened here in paradise.

Knowing my luck, the tabloids would get hold of this news, and I again would make the front page. And even though I hadn't heard from my Super Stalker Fan Club in nearly a month, I had a feeling they'd be making another appearance soon. How could they resist this?

Except for the fact that I had no connection to this crime. Nope. It was either random or maybe linked with the previous owner. But not me.

Thank goodness.

That was what I'd keep telling myself, at least.

I'd had my fill of real crime lately, and now I was ready to dive into the scripted variety.

I opened my eyes, glanced at my phone, and saw it was only noon. I'd planned on spending the day moving in and shopping. Granted, moving in for me meant unpacking six suitcases and unloading two bags of leftover groceries from the condo I'd been staying in.

The suitcases were sitting in the living room—Jackson had brought them in earlier. The rest of my belongings were enroute from California, where I'd put them in storage until I figured out my life.

Guess what? I figured out my life . . . and now this.

I let my head fall back against the house and closed my eyes.

In had been four weeks since the huge fiasco involving my mother and father. My mother, who just might be an international terrorist, was now missing. My father was in witness protection. At least I knew he was okay—which had been my whole reason for coming to this area. He'd disappeared, and I'd been fearful that something had happened to him.

It was now mid-July. Life had been a whirlwind since the showdown on Lantern Beach. I'd found out my TV series was being revived. I'd flown out to California to meet with my producer there. I'd come back and looked at houses, knowing I wanted to set up residence in this area. Then I'd had to fly back to LA for some early publicity. Then Jackson had gone to Raleigh to do some bomb tech training.

Things had been incredibly hectic.

And they still were.

As my hands ran across the wood beneath me, I paused. Something didn't feel right. I glanced down and saw something carved into the boards there.

I squinted. What did that say? The words were crude and hard to read. But it almost looked like it said, "I will be somebody."

What?

Who in the world would have carved those words? And why? Was this in some way related to the case? I had no idea, but I'd mention it to Jackson.

I replayed the moment I'd found the body inside. The woman had been on the younger side. Probably my age. She'd had brown hair that was cut to her shoulders.

To the best of my recollection, I'd never seen her before. I couldn't think of a single reason why she might be in my house. And I still had no idea if she'd been killed here or simply placed in my spare bedroom after she was already dead.

I mean, normally, I'd think the crime happened on scene. But nothing else here was torn up or gave any indication of a struggle. There was no blood. No pills. No rope. No nothing.

When your wheels spin like this, it usually leads to trouble, Joey.

And I didn't need any more trouble in my life.

I turned my head toward the house next door as a commotion there cut through the air.

I glanced across the dune at the place. It was a rental house. Most of the homes in this area were. The section of town where I'd purchased this house was an older area filled with large homes clad with cedar shingles, wooden hurricane shutters, massive decks, and tons of character.

I stared at the home beside me but didn't see anyone.

But there were clearly voices carrying outside.

Two heated, volatile voices.

I stood and edged closer to the noise. It almost sounded like the argument was coming from inside the house.

A man yelled something else—I couldn't make out his words but they sounded angry. A crash rattled the air.

A woman shouted back.

My muscles tensed.

Someone was having a big-time fight over there.

I waited, anxious to hear what would happen next. Anxious to know if I should call Jackson back over or grab one of the guys from inside to intercede.

I didn't want to be afraid to speak up—not if someone's life was in danger. And the good Lord knew after everything I'd been through that I didn't want someone to suffer with the same mistakes I'd made.

A moment later, the door slammed, and a man stormed out. I backed up, slipped behind a post, and turned, hoping it wouldn't be obvious I'd been watching.

But I was totally watching.

The man stomped toward his car, climbed inside, and pulled away with a loud screech of his tires.

A moment later, a woman slipped out the door and onto the deck. I didn't have to see her up close to notice the tears in her eyes. With her arms pulled tight across her chest, she gravitated toward the railing and stared out over the ocean.

What had just happened over there?

I nibbled on my bottom lip. Their fight was none of my business. I knew it wasn't. Yet I couldn't ignore the instant connection and sympathy I felt toward the woman.

The two of them had obviously had a fight. She didn't appear injured. That was good. At least, she wasn't injured *physically*. Emotionally it could be an entirely different story.

"Joey?" someone said behind me.

I turned to see the other officer at my door. I couldn't remember his real name, but I called him Officer Duck Donuts since I always saw him eating donuts from a local joint by the same name.

Jackson always joked about me and my bad memory—especially when it came to remembering things like passwords. He said I wouldn't be able to remember important details if my life depended on it.

"Yes?" I said.

"I'm all finished here. You're free to go inside. We're just asking that you don't go upstairs for the time being."

"No problem." I had no desire to go upstairs.

But now I had to figure out exactly what to do with myself since my visions of a happy move-in day had been ruined.

Okay, the last thing I wanted to do was go back into that house.

So I did what any respectable neighbor would do.

I went next door to introduce myself.

And *maybe* ask if the woman had seen anything over here in the past couple days.

And to feel her out to make sure she was okay.

The man she fought with hadn't returned yet, which made the timing perfect.

I twisted my hair into a bun as I hurried across the sand that separated my house from their rental. After straightening my blue short jumpsuit set and drawing in a deep breath, I knocked on the door.

A moment later, a pretty blonde with red-rimmed eyes cracked the door open. "Can I help you?"

The woman looked older than she should. I'd guess her to be in her mid-twenties, but her drawn features aged her. She had a slim build, long wavy hair, and a picture-perfect face.

"Hi, I'm Joey. I live next door." I pointed my thumb that way, trying to sound casual.

She squinted. "Is there a problem?"

"There was a little incident at my house, and I wondered if you'd seen anything. I'm assuming you probably checked in on Saturday or Sunday."

"What do you mean by *anything*?"

I remembered my earlier conversation with Jackson and knew I couldn't share specifics. "Any-thing suspicious?"

She opened the door wider, hugging her arms

around her. "I saw the police over there earlier. Is everything okay?"

"No, not really." I decided to go with the truth—just not all of it. "I just bought the house, but when I went inside, I discovered . . . someone had broken in. The whole place feels tainted now, you know?"

"I can imagine." She drew her arms even closer. "But I can't say I saw anything happen over there. Then again, I haven't been paying much attention."

"I understand. You and your husband are probably here on vacation, aren't you? I don't mean to ruin your fun here." Yep, I was fishing for information.

She frowned. "We are on vacation. We came down from Philadelphia. I'm Annie."

"Well, you picked a beautiful place to vacation, Annie. How do you like it so far?"

I was an actress, so this lighthearted banter façade should be a no-brainer, but every once in a while, things went south. At the heart of it all, I wanted to know that she was okay.

"Oh, it really is beautiful here. And I'm sorry to hear that something happened in your house. I really am. And I wish I could help. But I didn't see anything." Her hand was on the door, like she might close it.

She was trying to get rid of me, I realized.

That was when I zeroed in on a bruise on her arm.

Let it go, Joey. Let it go.

But I couldn't. I just couldn't, not based on my own past experiences.

I nodded toward the blemish. "Oh, man. What happened? Did you run into something?"

Annie reached for her bicep and covered the bruise. "Yes, I did. The door jam. I can be terribly clumsy sometimes."

I swallowed hard, wanting to call her out. But I couldn't. I didn't know her. I didn't have that kind of relationship.

Despite that, I swallowed hard and started, "Look, if you ever need—"

"Who do we have here?" someone asked beside me.

I froze at the deep tone. I didn't have to turn to know who it was. I recognized the voice from earlier.

It was Annie's other half.

CHAPTER
FOUR

I FORCED myself to plaster on a smile as I turned toward the man who'd stepped up beside me. He was large—well over six feet, with broad shoulders and a broad midsection. He had a head full of dark hair, cut short, and piercing eyes that dared me to challenge him.

I glanced at his hand and saw a paper bag with the top of a wine bottle protruding.

I cleared my throat and smiled broader, hoping to put him at ease. "Hey there. I'm your temporary neighbor while you're here in town. Name's Joey."

The man glared at me as he extended his hand. "I'm Adam."

"I was just asking your wife if she'd seen anything strange over at my house over the past day or two. She said she hadn't."

His dark gaze traveled to my place. "I'm not here to keep an eye on other people, just to enjoy myself."

"I understand." Yet the starkness of his words sent a shiver through me. I already didn't like this man. "I figured it was a longshot."

He narrowed his eyes, as if a memory hit him and some of his frostiness melted. "Actually, now that you mention it, there might be something."

"Anything would help." I stepped back and leaned against the railing. A slight sea breeze came from behind me, the smell of salty air along with it.

"Last night I saw a woman sitting on the deck. She looked like she belonged there—except for the fact that the house was all dark. People are weird, you know? I thought maybe she was decompressing."

"Did you say anything to her?"

He tersely shook his head. "No, I just nodded hello. She either didn't see me or she pretended like she didn't. Like I said, it didn't really matter to me. I'm not here to make friends—just to enjoy time with my wife." He raised the wine bottle.

When he did, Annie stepped forward and slipped her arms around his waist. The two looked happy—kind of. Actually, it looked like they were trying too hard.

"And this woman was just sitting there?" I clarified. "On my deck?"

"That's right. Almost like she was waiting for someone. She wasn't even sitting in a chair—just against the wall."

On the deck? Wait—was this the woman who'd carved the words there? I'd have to figure that out later. "Did she have chin-length brown hair, by chance?"

Adam let out a sigh, and I could tell I was testing his patience. "It was dark. I can't be sure."

"That was helpful. Thank you." I took a step away, my stomach churning. "And if you need anything while you're here, you know where to find me."

The last statement was directed toward Annie.

Adam continued to stare at me as I walked toward the stairs and back to my place.

That man was definitely dangerous. And Annie . . . she had all the signs of being in an abusive relationship. But I didn't know what to do to help her.

So I left, vowing to keep an ear open for any more trouble coming from the house next door. And if I needed to step in, I would.

Three hours later, I was dressed in a cute black sundress that flowed all the way down to my ankles and some strappy heels. I'd spent my time unpacking my suitcases. I had run to the store to get new sheets and pillows for myself. I was working under the assumption that I'd actually be able to sleep here tonight, though I wasn't entirely confident about that.

I'd still had a little time to kill, so I'd sat on my couch and read through my script. Then I looked through some missing persons reports, but I didn't see anyone who resembled the woman upstairs. I'd rounded out my time by watching funny cat videos. You could never go wrong with those.

At the moment, I was all ready for my big date with Jackson, and I couldn't wait to spend more time with him. And I really couldn't wait to get out of this house. In fact, I'd been on edge ever since the police left.

I couldn't stop thinking about that woman in the upstairs bedroom. It made no sense to me how she'd gotten into my house. Who she was. How she'd died.

The intrinsically nosy part of me wanted to check out the scene of the crime. Since only the upstairs was blocked off, I assumed that's where the crime scene was contained. And I could also only assume that the police had already checked the downstairs, trying to figure out if someone had broken in and left any clues on the way up to the bedroom.

As I pulled my feet beneath me, something rattled above me.

I froze.

What was that?

Not a ghost, Joey. Not a ghost. Ghosts aren't real.

I waited, desperate to know if I'd hear the noise again. Everything was silent. Eerily silent.

I released my breath. The sound had been nothing. I'd probably just imagined it, for that matter.

I relaxed against the cushions.

Until I heard the sound again.

It was definitely a rattle. Directly above me.

Above me?

Was that the location of the bedroom where we'd found the dead woman?

I could hardly breathe again.

Maybe the woman was haunting this place.

Ghosts aren't real. Ghosts aren't real.

I didn't care. I had to get out of this house.

I glanced at the time on my phone. It was 5:30. Jackson should be here any minute. Thank goodness.

I decided to wait for him on the deck. As soon as I closed the door behind me, I breathed easier. I felt suffocated in my own house. That was never a good sign.

Deep in my gut, I knew that, until I had answers about what had happened inside, I would never have any peace about staying here.

But I was going to let Jackson find those answers.

In theory.

No, I should resolve to stay out of it.

But getting involved was so tempting.

I leaned over the deck and breathed deeply. It was two stories to the ground. All the houses here—most of them, at least—were built on stilts to combat the ocean's overwash and flooding concerns. Sand stretched below.

Just looking down caused a wave of dizziness to come over me. I'd never been one for heights, but around here you had to get used to them. Just for good measure, I shook the railing. It felt steady—thank goodness.

My gaze traveled to the house next to mine. All had been quiet since I'd heard the fight earlier today. Maybe the two of them had shared some wine and made up.

I still shuddered as I thought about someone living with that kind of anger. It wasn't fun or healthy. I prayed it was a one-time thing, but I knew better.

I glanced at the time again before pacing around to the other side of the deck—the side closest to my driveway, where I could see Jackson when he arrived. But as I stepped that way, something else caught my eye.

It was a woman. Hiding in the dune grass near my house.

And staring at me like a UFO hunter who'd just seen a mysterious light in the sky.

CHAPTER
FIVE

I SUCKED IN A DEEP BREATH.

The woman didn't have a camera—not a visible one, at least.

Was she a fan trying to catch a glimpse of me so she could tell her friends about it?

Maybe. It *had* happened before.

But I didn't get that impression.

What if she was here because of the dead body? Were the two events related?

I needed to find out.

"Hey, wait!" I started toward the stairs so I could catch her and talk.

Of course that didn't work.

The woman took off down my driveway, headed toward the sidewalk that led along the beach road.

And, of course, I decided to follow her.

In my heels.

Please don't let the paparazzi see this . . .

Running in high heels was much more difficult in real life than it was on camera. No detective with an ounce of self-preservation should wear these.

But, in my gut, I knew this woman had answers. And I needed answers if I was ever going to be able to sleep in this house.

How did I know? Easy. A fan would stick around for an autograph. Would be flattered that I'd called her out and given her an opportunity to interact. The fact that this woman ran showed some kind of internal guilt.

My legs burned—and wobbled—as I headed down my steps, to my driveway, and to the sidewalk.

The woman was fast—much faster than I was. But that wasn't going to stop me. I pushed myself down the sidewalk, despite the strange looks I was getting from tourists in bathing suits with floats around their midsections.

A Jeep pulled out from a public parking area, stopped and waited for traffic to clear before turning. The woman slowed so she wouldn't crash into it. She glanced behind her.

Her eyes widened when she saw me gaining on her.

The topless Jeep took off, and the woman skirted around it.

But not before grabbing something from the back.

A beach umbrella.

Before I realized what was happening, she opened it and propelled it behind her.

Right toward me.

The breeze caught it and sent it flying like a bullet disguised as a rainbow. The tip hit me in the chest and the rest of it hit the rest of me. I raised my hands and slapped the cheerful stripes from my face.

Finally, it flew behind me.

I scowled when I saw that the woman had gained considerable ground and speed.

But I wasn't giving up yet.

I hiked up my dress and kicked up my effort to a new level that I didn't know I had.

As I reached another parking lot, two vehicles pulled out, waiting to turn and so close I couldn't get between them.

Traffic around this time of year . . .

I didn't have time to wait for them to move.

Instead, I put my foot on the tire of the first vehicle—a truck—and climbed over the bed.

"Hey!" the driver yelled.

"Sorry," I called behind me.

Then I kept going.

The woman stopped. Saw what I'd done. Her eyes widened again and then she kept running.

But her pause had been just what I needed.

I was close enough that if I lunged . . .

Without thinking through any repercussions, I threw myself toward her.

My body flew through the air for just a split second until finally my hands caught the woman's shoulders. We both tumbled onto the sandy ground beside the sidewalk.

But not before my ankle twisted.

Again.

I paused and bit back my pain.

Because I had her. I'd caught her.

And now I wanted answers.

"Please, let me go." The woman struggled under me, her hair thrashing over her face. "I didn't do anything."

I grabbed her arms, trying to restrain her—just like I'd learned to do while acting out many scenes on my show. It couldn't be much different in real life.

Only she put up more of a struggle than the actors on the set.

"Why did you run?" I asked through clenched teeth.

"Because you scared me." She continued to fight me, her body in motion as she tried to get away.

"I scared you?" I hadn't heard that one before.

The woman stopped struggling and looked at me. Her eyes widened. "Oh. My. Goodness. You're Joey Darling? Joey Darling just tackled me."

I didn't know if I should feel good about myself that she'd recognized me or if I should run. "That's right. You were outside my house. Staring at me."

"No, I was staring at the house."

"Why would you stare at the house?"

"Because my friend was last seen there. And, until now, I didn't understand why."

CHAPTER
SIX

BEFORE I COULD PULL myself off the woman,
a truck pulled up beside us, and I heard a confused,
"Joey?"

I glanced over and saw Jackson there staring at us
with a look of flabbergastion—yes, I'd made up that
word, but I loved it—on his face.

He pulled to the side of the road and hopped out.

"Hi, honey." I kept one hand on the woman,
afraid she might run.

"What in the world . . . ?" He quickly reached us
and leaned down to help me up—actually, it was
more like to pull me off the woman.

As soon as I put weight on my ankle, pain ricocheted through me.

"Don't lose her," I said through gritted teeth,
scowling at the intruder who was still on the grass

beside the sidewalk. The woman was probably in her late twenties. She was painfully thin, with strawberry blonde hair that brushed her shoulders and pale skin.

Jackson's gaze went to the woman. He still looked confused, and rightfully so. A circle of people surrounded us, watching and probably recording the whole incident on their cell phones.

Score another one for Joey, the queen of disaster and ill-gotten publicity.

"Who is she? And are you okay?" Jackson's gaze narrowed with either concern or confusion or quite possibly both.

"I'll be fine." My ankle felt anything but fine right now. But I couldn't pay attention to that. No, I had to make sure this woman didn't get away. If she tried, I would spring into action, even if it meant enduring more pain. "This woman knows something about what happened at my house, and she was spying on me on my property."

Jackson stepped toward the bush-hiding, rainbow-umbrella-throwing secret keeper and helped her to her feet. "Maybe we should go somewhere to discuss this—and to get you off your ankle."

She stood, scowling and wiping sand from her jean shorts, legs, elbows, and everywhere else. Finally, with a huff, she straightened and gave me a death glare. "I'm not going anywhere with you two. Are you crazy?"

Jackson sighed and pulled out his badge. "Detective Jackson Sullivan. I need a moment of your time."

"I don't have anything to say."

She started to step away, clearly blowing Jackson off, when he grabbed her arm, lightly but firmly. "Ma'am, we're investigating a murder."

Her eyes widened. "A . . . a murder?"

"Do you have information that might help us?"

She shook her head in quick, frantic motions. "I . . . I don't know. I don't think so. Should I?"

Jackson glanced around. The crowd surrounding us was clearly using us as their afternoon entertainment. "There's nothing to see here, people. Please enjoy your vacations. Enjoy the beach. But don't enjoy this scene."

After some murmuring, the tourists dispersed.

I leaned against Jackson's truck, trying to get the weight off my ankle. I took off my heels and stepped right on—what else? A sand spur.

I bit back a mutter of pain and yanked nature's torture device from my foot.

I couldn't win today.

"Listen, we can sit in my truck or we can go somewhere," Jackson said. "Maybe even the police station. But we need to talk."

It was a good thing Jackson had shown up, because I was in no state to interrogate someone right now. My ankle hurt, as well as my elbow. Plus, I couldn't catch my breath and my heart still raced out of control.

Being a detective in real life was much harder than being a detective on TV.

That was a lesson I should have learned already. And I had. But I'd forgotten. Or, at least I'd put the hard stuff out of my mind.

"Fine." The woman's gaze flashed from Jackson to me. "But I'll only talk at the house. I need some answers also."

Ten minutes later, we were seated on my couch. Wesley's couch, actually. We just needed a thick desk, some homey plants, ink-blot artwork, and a man with a nonjudgmental gaze sitting across from us as we talked and this really would look like a therapist's office.

Against my better instincts, I'd pulled out some Izzes—my favorite drink—and offered one to the strange woman who'd been spying on me. I wished I knew if I was offering a friend or an enemy a drink.

I hardly had time to worry about it—my ankle still hurt. I put some ice on it and propped it up on the couch beside me. I didn't think it was sprained. I think I'd simply exacerbated an old injury.

"Let's start with your name." Jackson sat in a

chair across from the woman I'd tackled, his body posed with professional interest in the situation.

"Jennifer Walton."

Her nose was red and her eyes were rimmed in pink. I wasn't sure if this was her normal look or if she was upset and flushed. Maybe it was a mix of both.

"Ms. Walton, why were you outside Joey's house watching her?" Jackson asked.

She absently rubbed the side of her drink and sighed, looking all-together annoyed. "I was looking for my friend, Desiree. This whole thing has nothing to do with murder."

Desiree? Was that the name of the woman who'd been found dead in the room upstairs? "Why would you think Desiree was here?"

"It was the last location where her phone pinged. Now that I know you live here, it makes sense."

I shook my head, wondering what that meant exactly. Was Desiree the woman Adam had seen on my deck? Was she the person who'd carved the words there?

"Please go on," I said, anxious to hear more.

Jennifer sighed again. "My friend Desiree wants to be an actress. She *is* an actress—just not a well-known one. She's done some commercials. A small indie film. She's worked as an extra." Jennifer's gaze connected with mine. "She was just down in Wilmington auditioning for a role in the renewed *Relentless* season."

My eyebrows shot up at the unexpected connection to me. Earlier, I'd assumed that this murder had nothing to do with me. Apparently, I was wrong. "Was she?"

"She found out she didn't make the cut, though." Jennifer shrugged. "She was devastated. Desperate, I guess. I suppose you remember what that was like, Joey. How hard it is to get your big break."

I did know that, yet I didn't. I'd stumbled into acting, catching my big break without much effort, a fact I didn't take lightly. No, I'd seen too many people trying to sell their souls to achieve what they considered the ultimate life—fame and fortune.

I'd learned that neither of those things were what they were cracked up to be. What really mattered was spending time with the people you cared about, doing work that brought satisfaction, and giving back to others—by doing things like helping find answers for them about crimes that haunted them, for example.

"I'm still not sure how that led her here," I said, trying to put the pieces together.

Jennifer picked a piece of lint off a navy-blue pillow beside her before looking back at us. "She heard you were living here in the Outer Banks now. I mean, it's all over the tabloids, right?"

"It is?" I blurted.

"Of course. *The National Instigator* ran a story on it last week. They even announced that you were buying a house."

I had no idea. How had I missed that? And how had the *Instigator* found out?

Those people. . . I was their favorite fodder. And that wasn't necessarily a good thing.

"Anyway, Desiree wanted to find you and convince you to give her a role," Jennifer continued. "She said if she could just talk to you, you'd know that she was meant to be in your show."

"I don't really have that power."

"I know that. But, like I said, she was desperate."

"So she came here to find Joey," Jackson repeated. "And try and convince her to give her a role on *Relentless*. And now you're here?"

Jennifer nodded, her eyes so wide they were almost comical and, with her nose still red, almost like she had a cold. "I haven't heard from her in twenty-four hours. She texts me all the time. We're like sisters. In fact, we put those apps on our phones that lets us track each other. So I tracked her to this address about sixteen hours ago. I live in Atlanta, so it took me a while to get here. And after I arrived, I had no idea whose home this was. I only knew it was the last place Desiree had been."

"Good to know," Jackson said.

Jennifer looked back and forth between the two of us. "So have you seen her? Did she come here to talk?"

My gut squeezed as the truth hit me. Jackson and I exchanged a glance. Finally, Jackson spoke.

"Do you have a picture of Desiree?" He sounded like he'd chosen his words carefully.

"Of course." Jennifer searched her phone before holding the device up. "Here she is."

I sucked in a quick breath at the image of a smiling, happy, very much alive woman.

She was clearly the same person we'd found upstairs in my house.

Jennifer had no idea her best friend was dead.

And now we were going to have to tell her.

I *so* never wanted to be a real-life detective, mostly for moments like this.

CHAPTER
SEVEN

ONCE THE DAM HAD OPENED, Jennifer talked and talked. For an entire hour. Telling Jackson and me more than we needed to know, really. About Desiree's favorite food—hot dogs, in case you were wondering. About her aspirations—to be famous, of course. About her larger-than-life personality—and only someone with that kind of personality would have the nerve to track me down and beg for a role in my TV show.

I'd joked earlier that my couch looked like it belonged in a therapy office.

Little did I know that it would be a self-fulfilling prophecy.

I had learned a few helpful details, however. Desiree Williams was twenty-three years old. She was originally from a small Mississippi town, but she'd moved to Atlanta—which did have a growing presence in the TV and film industry—right out of high school.

That was where she'd met Jennifer, who also wanted to be an actress. However, Jennifer had gone to college and gotten a degree in teaching to pay her bills until she found her big break. She'd also discovered that she liked teaching, so getting her big break had become less important.

Desiree, on the other hand, took odd jobs to pay her bills. Getting her big break was all she could think about. She was desperate to be someone, even though she already was someone. Fame didn't—or shouldn't, at least—define people.

I sighed and leaned back on my couch, my mental wheels still spinning. Jackson had left an hour ago to take Jennifer to the police station so she could identify the body. She was a shaking, trembling mess.

I'd offered to go also as moral support, but Jennifer had declined.

Did she blame me for her friend's death?

It was a possibility.

Maybe Jennifer thought if Desiree had never come here she'd still be alive.

I didn't really know.

I pulled my legs underneath me, the house's presence pressing on me. While Jennifer had been here, I'd been distracted from the horrible event that had occurred here, but now that I was alone, I was all too aware of how quiet it was.

A pounding sound cut through the air, and I jumped off the couch, making a mental note to add "Ghostbusters" to my speed dial number. Okay, they weren't real. But I could program their song as my ringtone. That always made everything better.

"Joey, it's me. Jackson."

I released my breath. Jackson. It was just Jackson. Knocking at the door.

Not a ghost from the afterlife haunting me.

I rushed toward the door and opened it, desperate to confirm it was really him.

It was.

He rubbed my arm as he stepped inside. "How are you doing, Joey?"

"I've been better. Been worse."

"That's understandable."

I closed the door but didn't move from the spot. "How did it go down at the station?"

"About as well as you can imagine. Jennifer is devastated. She confirmed that it was Desiree we found upstairs."

"So what's next?"

Jackson shrugged. "We contact Desiree's family. See if they have any information. Now that we know her name, we can trace her financials. Check her social media."

"That's a good start, at least."

Jackson studied my face a minute before asking, "I know a lot has happened. You still want to go grab dinner?"

I glanced at the time. It was already 7:30. "Everywhere will be packed."

"I'm willing to wait if you are."

That was sweet of Jackson. I appreciated that he wanted to make me a priority. But . . . "I'm not feeling up to anything fancy. How about we go to the fish market and grab some super unhealthy fried seafood and go sit on the beach to eat it?"

He squinted. "I thought you weren't eating gluten?"

"I changed my mind. Just for today at least."

He grinned. "Okay then. Something low-key sounds really good to me also."

Thirty minutes later, we were settled at the base of a sand dune with Styrofoam containers in our laps. Jackson still wore his button-up shirt and jeans. I still wore my flowy black sundress. Both of us were barefoot and probably a sight to behold.

That wasn't to mention my ankle. It was sore, but I could still walk on it. I just had to watch my step.

"I love this about you, Joey," Jackson said.

"Love what? That I break my diet every week?"

He chuckled. "That you could be stuck-up and snooty, but instead you're down to earth and casual.

You're okay with a romantic dinner out of Styrofoam containers."

"Anything with you, I'm okay with." I smiled. And I meant it.

His eyes were warm on mine, as if he appreciated my words, before he turned back to enjoy the landscape around us.

Colors of dusk still smeared this side of the island, even though the sun set behind us. Soothing pinks and pale blues stretched in wisps across the sky and added a lovely shading to the ocean.

Most of the crowds had left by now, but there were still a few families and a couple fishermen.

I picked up a salty fry, knowing I'd regret this meal later. "I know we shouldn't talk about your cases when we're out enjoying the evening. But can I have five minutes, at least?"

"Five minutes seems fair, considering the circumstances."

My heart pulsed a beat with excitement. Jackson was throwing me a bone, and I would happily take it. "Okay, is there anything you can tell me that Jennifer told you?"

Jackson took a bite of his fried flounder. The scent of the crispy batter subtly wafted toward me, mingling with the salty ocean air. It might not seem like the perfect scent combination, but it was. Especially when mixed with the gritty feel of the sand beneath my bare feet.

"You heard most of it. At least we can now ID the victim. But there's still a lot that doesn't make sense."

"That's what I think too. I mean, sure, Desiree came to my house to see me. What happened between the time she arrived and the time we found her?"

"That's a great question. We're estimating she died last night."

I sucked in a breath, realizing I hadn't told him important stuff that I needed to tell him. "My neighbor saw a woman sitting on my deck last night."

"When did you hear that?"

"A little earlier." But I wasn't done yet. "And I found a message carved into one of the wood planks. It said, 'I will be somebody.'"

"You think Desiree left it there?"

"It fits, doesn't it? And the carved letters looked fresh, you know?" I popped another fried shrimp into my mouth.

"I'll need to take a look at that. But it fits. Desiree was at your house last night, hanging out and waiting for you to return. Something happened and she ended up dead and inside."

I wiped my greasy fingers on a paper napkin and

turned to Jackson. "You gathered that from talking to Jennifer?"

Jackson shrugged and picked up another french fry. "I gathered that from talking to various people, including the medical examiner."

"I see."

"Who knows what happened?" Jackson stared ahead. "Maybe Desiree ran into trouble—stumbled into a random crime—just outside your house. Maybe the killer knew the house was vacant and placed her inside, hoping to buy himself some time until she was discovered."

"Where was she even staying? I mean, I heard everything in town is booked at this time of year."

"We don't know yet. Her car was found about an hour ago at a public beach access not far from your place. We wonder if she was sleeping there at night."

"Part of me feels guilty that we're not investigating right now—"

"We're?"

I shrugged, realizing I hadn't watched my words. "You're?"

"You have enough on your plate, Joey. Let me handle this."

"But you don't understand. I don't think I can even sleep in that place tonight."

"Of course you can."

"Of course maybe I *can't*. And if I can't sleep, I'll

get bags under my eyes. Then I'll start eating to stay awake. Then I'll gain weight. Then I'll get cranky. No one wants a cranky Joey. And this is terrible timing because the camera will capture all of those imperfections and amplify them by 100 percent. Then the tabloids will pick up on it, and they'll start theorizing. They might ask if I'm pregnant or—"

"Joey." Jackson placed his hand on my knee. "You're going to be fine."

I waited a moment for his words to wash over me, and then I released my breath. "You're right. I will be."

And I believed that for all of two seconds. Until my phone buzzed.

It was the moving company. Their truck had crashed, and all of my things were now on the side of the road somewhere in Texas.

CHAPTER
EIGHT

I FINISHED MY MEAL—I only ate half of it, but it was enough.

I placed the container back in the paper bag, took a long sip of water, and then looked out over the ocean. The pinks and blues had both deepened, and gray had started to fade from overhead.

"Insurance will cover the replacement costs of your things," Jackson said.

He was right. This was just one more thing piled on top of an already long list of headaches in my life right now. "I know it's just stuff. I guess I'm feeling a bit overwhelmed."

"I'm sorry." He squeezed my knee. "I know the road hasn't been exactly smooth lately."

"Not in the least."

We sat there for a few minutes in silence. Everything had been going okay for the past month—until I found that dead body upstairs. Maybe it was a bad omen. Like rain on your wedding day. Or a black cat crossing your path.

Finding a dead body in your new home had to mean something, right?

I mean, not that I was superstitious . . . except maybe sometimes I was. Or, at least, I wondered if superstitious folklore might be true. Because it *seemed* true.

I had to figure out what happened to Desiree. Maybe if I did, I would end this unlucky streak that had started and then snowballed out of control.

"Joey?" Jackson murmured.

"Yes?"

"I just want you to know . . . I don't want to date anyone else."

My eyes widened at the serious tone of his voice. "You don't want to what?"

"To date anyone else." He shrugged. "I know we've been dating for a while now. But we've never really talked about us. And what 'us' is. If we're exclusive or just having fun or—"

Jackson wasn't the type to just have fun, so that thought had never crossed my mind.

"So you want me to be your girl?" I teased.

He grinned back at me. "Yeah, something like that."

I leaned forward and planted a kiss on his lips. "Jackson Sullivan, I would love nothing more than to be your girl."

His lips covered mine again. "I'm glad to hear it. I love you, Joey."

"I love you too, Jackson."

Maybe this day wasn't so bad after all. Even with the dead body.

Jackson and I had stayed on the beach for another hour. I'd rested my head on his shoulder, and he'd put his arm around my waist. We'd talked about ordinary, normal things.

The moment had felt like pure bliss—pure, simple bliss.

I felt like I was glowing and floating—in other words, I could be radioactive. Or I could be over-the-moon happy and in love.

I couldn't stop thinking about Jackson and how much I loved him.

All of this was almost enough to distract me from the fact that there had been a dead woman in my house.

We'd finally headed back to my place, but we didn't go any farther than the deck. Instead, as we stood in front of each other, I stepped closer, still amazed that this man was mine.

Jackson ran his thumb over my cheek. "I love you, Joey Darling."

"I love you too, Jackson Sullivan."

He didn't say it, but I think he feared something would change when I left to begin filming. And he had every right to be scared.

Not because I would leave him.

But filming could be a breeding ground for less-than-ideal relationship conditions.

Jackson and I would be away from each other. It would definitely be a test of our relationship.

Part of me dreaded having these simple times end. I'd been on a break from Hollywood since I'd been here for the last six months. But I'd been on a break before that also. After my husband had nearly killed me, I'd had rehab. I'd been trying to pull my life together. I'd been unable to find work.

And did I mention that I'd been bankrupt?

There had been some dark days.

They were behind me. But there would be challenges ahead.

The filming schedule could be grueling. Twelve-hour days. Working weekends sometimes.

We had eighteen episodes. That would equal eighteen weeks. I hoped to make it home on weekends. Or that Jackson could swing down and see me.

As Jackson's lips met mine, those worries became a distant memory.

Until I heard yelling.

I froze and listened. It was coming from my neighbors' house.

Again.

CHAPTER
NINE

JACKSON'S GAZE followed mine and his brow furrowed as the argument intensified. "What's going on over there?"

I sighed as the noise of the fight broke the otherwise blissful moment. "They were fighting like that earlier."

Jackson glanced back at me. "Are they just yelling?"

"I don't know. I didn't see anything physical, but I suspect there's more to this. After all, I am an excellent reader of people."

Jackson's gaze narrowed. "Are you?"

"I'm an actress. I study body language. I think that pretty much makes me an expert."

"Good to know."

Annie's voice cut through the air. "I didn't even want to come here!"

"This was supposed to bring us closer together," Adam yelled back.

"I've never wanted to be farther away from you than now!"

Jackson grimaced, and an uncomfortable silence passed. Hearing two people who'd once been in love fighting like that was definitely a killjoy. Jackson seemed to read my thoughts, and he pulled me into a hug—a hug that seemed to promise that we'd never be that couple.

"I guess you can't do anything," I murmured into his chest.

"Yelling isn't a crime. Now, if he threatens her or raises a hand to her . . . that's a different story."

"I feel so bad for them." More of my warm fuzzy feelings disappeared as the yelling continued.

Then something crashed.

Jackson stiffened. "I'm going to go check things out."

As he walked toward my neighbors' house, I followed him. But I'd stay a good distance away when he talked to them. I mean, I couldn't just stand here and do nothing.

So I stayed around the corner. Lingering between out of sight and out in the open. I'd choose which one when the time came.

Jackson pounded at the door. Footsteps stomped.

A moment later, the door opened, and a man said, "Can I help you?"

"Detective Jackson Sullivan. I heard a disturbance inside the house and wanted to check to see if everything was okay."

"Everything's fine." The words sounded short and clipped.

When I heard the tension in Adam's voice, I definitely decided to stay out of sight. I pressed myself into the wall, just around the corner, and listened. As I did, I tried to picture the scene in my head. Was Adam's face red with anger? Was Annie cowering inside?

And Jackson. . . I didn't have to imagine. I knew him well enough to know that he was bristled with tension yet professional.

"I'd like to check inside your house to confirm that."

"It's fine," Adam said. "My wife and I just had an argument. It was nothing life-threatening or any reason for concern."

"I heard something crash," Jackson continued.

"That was me." I recognized Annie's voice. "I got mad and threw a dish. But no one is hurt. Our emotions just got the best of us."

Was that the truth? I doubted it.

"Can I talk to you outside alone, ma'am?" Jackson asked.

"That won't be necessary." Adam sounded angry, like he'd said the words through clenched teeth.

"I'd like your wife to speak for herself."

"I'm fine," Annie said. "I really am. Look at me. Everything is good."

I wanted to look at her. I really did. But I didn't dare peer out. I had a feeling I'd mess everything up if I did, like I'd disturb some kind of delicate balance.

Uncomfortable silence stretched.

"If you need anything, give me a call," Jackson said. "Or if the two of you need time apart to cool off, I'd suggest you do that. I'd hate to have to pay another visit here."

"You won't have to," Adam said. "Thank you for your concern."

He sounded like he was seething, though.

A moment later, Jackson joined me, took my elbow, and led me away, not saying anything until we reached my house.

I thought he might scold me for following him without clearing it first. But he didn't. Instead, he shook his head.

"What's wrong?" I asked.

His jaw flexed. "I don't like what's going on over there."

"I don't either. I guess there's nothing you can do?"

"I didn't witness anything. It's unfortunate because until the wife reports something or someone is injured, my hands are tied."

We paused by the front door, and I didn't know what else to say. He was right—his hands were tied, and there was nothing I could do either except try to keep an eye on the situation.

But maybe—just maybe—Jackson and I could have a moment of normalcy. Maybe I could try and forget everything that had gone wrong. Try to forget Desiree.

"Listen, I know a lot has happened, but do you want to come in for a second? Maybe unwind a little?"

"I'd love to." Just as he said the words, his phone rang. He looked at the screen and frowned. "Except I've got to go check out a domestic disturbance. Something must be in the air tonight."

My heart sank.

This wasn't the way I wanted my evening to end.

"I understand," I told him. Because I did understand. Jackson had a job to do, and he couldn't always control his hours.

"I'll call later?"

"That sounds great." But as he stepped away, I called to him again.

He paused and turned toward me. "Yes?"

"I know this is going to sound strange, but . . . can we keep our relationship between the two of us?" I held my breath as I waited for his response.

His eyes narrowed. "What do you mean?"

"That didn't come out right," I quickly explained. "There's nothing more that I want to do than announce this to the world. But as soon as reporters catch wind of this . . . they're going to be hounding me for information. I'm not ready to share this news with the world yet. I just want to enjoy you and me without all of the craziness."

"So you're not going to tell people we're official?" His voice rose with confusion.

I could tell by Jackson's expression that he didn't like that idea. His lips were drawn, his brow furrowed, his shoulders even looked tight.

"Jackson—" I started, desperate to offer some kind of balm to the situation.

He took a step back. "If that's what you think you need to do for a little while, I understand. I guess I just want to shout how much I love you from the rooftops, not hide it."

"It's not that I want to hide it. I just want to treasure it. I know it sounds weird. But I just want to keep some things private. Please don't think this has anything to do with you."

He planted a quick kiss on my lips. "We can talk more later. I really do need to go now."

I watched him walk away, wishing he didn't have to leave. But he did.

And I had to stay.

Stay in this house tainted by crime.

Dread pooled in my stomach. I didn't want to do this. But I had no choice.

I needed something to distract myself because sitting alone in this house wasn't cutting it for me.

I mean, sure, I could marvel all I wanted about how happy I was to be in a new and serious relationship. And I *was* happy. Deliriously so. But all those warm fuzzy feelings were overridden by the memories of finding the body upstairs. This whole place felt tainted now, and I couldn't relax.

Maybe I should have called my friend Phoebe to see if I could stay with her this evening.

But no, I had to try and act all tough about it. Like a grownup. Like an independent, self-sufficient woman.

Those things were way overrated sometimes.

Instead, I sat on my couch, wearing my most comfortable pajamas, and grabbed my phone.

I might as well make myself useful, right?

Even though it was ten at night, I called my producer, Mark Johnson. I knew he'd be awake since he was a night owl.

He answered on the first ring. "Joey, my girl. What's going on? You working on memorizing that script?"

"Of course." I'd read it through. That counted as memorizing it, right? The beginning stages of it, at least. "I can't wait to get started next week."

"Neither can we. We've been given a second chance. I think this will be a good move."

"I do too." I shifted. "Listen, I have a question for you. I know you like to sit in on all the auditions, correct?"

"That's right. Why?"

"Do you remember a woman named Desiree Williams who auditioned for a role as secretary?"

"Desiree, you said?"

"That's right. She was a petite brunette—"

"Yes, I remember her. But why are you asking? I've already given that role to someone else."

He remembered her. That had to be significant, right? He'd probably had hundreds of auditions this weekend. "Why didn't she get the role?"

"Desiree was a decent actress, but it was clear to me that she was high-maintenance. I didn't want someone who needed to be coddled or who tried to be controlling. She had that written all over her. So I gave the role to someone who was laid-back but equally as talented."

That made sense. "I see. Do you remember anything about her audition? Like, why did you think she was high-maintenance? Usually an actress only has a few minutes with you, so those are a lot of conclusions to draw."

"Oh, it was obvious. Really obvious. She wanted a do-over with her audition. We said no. She looked upset. She broke down and said she needed this role, acting like her life depended on it. She said she had no money for groceries."

Hmm . . . emotional manipulation? Possibly. Desperation? Definitely. All together it was bad form for an audition, however.

"A lot of actors and actresses find themselves tight on money," Mark continued. "But an audition is no place to beg for sympathy. We're not a nonprofit. We need to pick the best people we can. You know that. Why are you asking?"

I explained to Mark what had happened.

"What?" His voice rose with surprise. "That's insane."

"I know. When was the audition again? I can't keep the timeline straight."

"It was just this past week. I announced who got roles on Saturday. She must have left right after that to hunt you down. Be glad you hadn't moved into the house yet. Who knows? Maybe she would have been the type to hold a gun to your head until you met her ransom demands."

A shiver raked through me. It wasn't too late. Could Desiree still hunt me down, even in death? "Not comforting."

"Well, she's dead now. I wouldn't worry about it too much."

"Yeah, she's dead all right. She was found dead in my new house. Draw your own conclusions."

He clucked his tongue. "I'm sensing some new ideas for an upcoming episode of *Relentless*."

"Very funny." I scowled, even though I could very well see the whole situation playing out onscreen. If I wasn't living it, it would be entertaining.

"No, really—I'm sorry that happened and that you were pulled into it," Mark said. "This could be a great press angle, though—"

"No press," I said. I'd had enough of that. As much as I wanted this reboot to succeed, I wouldn't sell my soul—or privacy—to make it happen.

"Got it. Okay, I'll see you soon, Joey. Be safe. If Desiree comes to visit you from the afterlife, tell her there's an upcoming role for a ghost in *Relentless*."

I scowled again and grabbed a blanket from behind the couch, suddenly feeling chilled. "You're just so funny today."

"I try! Night."

As soon as I hung up, a knock sounded at my door.

Who could possibly be coming over at this hour? It was 10:30, for goodness sake. And, after everything that had happened, did I really want to find out?

I had no idea.

CHAPTER
TEN

AGAINST MY BETTER INSTINCTS, I walked toward the door. I paused, unsure if I wanted to even open it.

And then I heard, "Joey? You there? It's me."

What? Was that . . .?

I opened the door, and Sam Butler stood there, leaning against the door frame and looking 100 percent Hollywood. Cue the audience applause track.

And that applause track would be well deserved. Sam was a noted Hollywood leading man with his broad shoulders, broader smile, and charismatic personality.

Before I could say anything, he pulled me into a hug, lifting me and turning in circles.

"*Relentless* is coming back on!" He placed me back on my feet. "Can you believe it?"

"I know! And you're . . . here. In Nags Head. Right now." What in the world was Sam doing? Had I missed an email or text message?

"Yes, I am." He stepped inside and glanced around. "Nice house, by the way."

"Thanks." I closed the door and stared at him. "What a surprise to see you here."

He was my *Relentless* costar. He played a brooding ex-CIA officer who was as tough as nails. In real life, he was fun and the life of the party. And he was a good friend . . . kind of. I mean, when we were together, we had chemistry. We had fun.

But when we were apart . . . I doubted either of us really thought of the other. He did, however, let me stay at his place for a while after Eric and I had split. I'd be forever indebted to him for that.

"It's been a while so I figured we should reconnect and maybe rehearse together," Sam said.

I crossed my arms and leaned against the wall, trying to figure out how to broach this subject. "I see. I . . . I hadn't planned on any of this, however."

He picked up a sea star from the table beside him and absently studied it. "I know you. You're always up for a good time."

I held back a sigh. I thought I'd grown up since then. I *hoped* I'd grown up since then. But what if I hadn't? What if the changes in me were because of this place? Because of the people I was around? Would I be strong enough to remain this new person once I was back around old influences again?

I desperately wanted to say yes.

But I wasn't totally sure.

"I am," I finally responded. "It's just that . . . I wish I could have planned. And how did you find me?"

"I just did a Google search. This address came up. In fact, there were three cars driving past and taking pictures when I pulled up. It looks like everyone knows you bought this place. Hopefully you weren't looking for privacy."

"I was." How had I been discovered? I really hoped I didn't have to hire security . . . unless Jackson counted.

If that was the case, fans could drive by all they wanted. As long as Jackson was nearby to keep me safe, it would be a good trade-off.

Sam plopped on the couch. "You look great, by the way."

"Thanks. So do you. I'm surprised Hank didn't come."

"Hank? Didn't you hear? He's dating Kate Hatchet now."

My eyes widened. "Kate Hatchet? I had no idea."

"Oh, yeah. The two seem really happy together."

"Well, good for him. And you?" I lowered myself in a chair across from him. I might as well make the best of this since Sam was here and obviously not going anywhere.

"I've just been taking it easy. I did that film for HBO—*Hood Links*. Did you see it?"

"No, but I heard about it. You were nominated for an award, right?"

"Golden Globe."

"That's awesome. Good for you."

We talked for two more hours until my eyelids started to droop. And then I rose.

"You get a hotel room in town?" I asked.

Sam shrugged. "No, I thought I'd crash here. Besides, I heard some people at the gas station saying that all the hotels are booked. Is it okay that I stay? I didn't think you'd mind."

My stomach clenched. Here? Oh no. How did I tell my friend—and that's all we'd ever been—that it would be weird for him to stay with me? Especially when there was nowhere else to stay.

"The upstairs is off-limits right now, so that would only leave the couch . . ." That seemed like a good way to broach the subject and gently discourage him. I mean, who wanted to sleep on a couch?

"I'm good with that. I'll go grab my things."

I bit down on my bottom lip. A few months ago, I

wouldn't have thought anything about this. But now?

I had my doubts that this was a good idea. A lot of doubts. Especially now that I was officially Jackson's girlfriend.

As Sam settled on the couch, I excused myself into my bedroom and called Jackson.

Though part of me said Sam staying here wasn't a big deal, the other part put myself in Jackson's shoes. What if he had a girl spend the night at his place? Would I be jealous? Oh, yeah. I wouldn't be happy at all. I wanted to be respectful of our relationship. But where did that leave my friendship with Sam?

Unease churned in my gut as I waited for him to answer. I sat on the bed—not *my* bed but at least I'd changed the sheets and comforter—and I crossed my legs beneath me. I could really use some familiar comforts right now, but instead I felt like I was living in a stranger's house.

"Hey, what's going on?" Jackson answered. "It's late."

Based on the murmuring in the background, he was still working the case.

How did I say this? I just needed to get it all out at once. "My old friend from *Relentless* surprised me and showed up in town. He's staying at my place. I just wanted to let you know."

The words came out rapid fire.

"Wait. What did you say? A guy is staying over at your house?"

And there it was. I could already hear in Jackson's tone that he didn't like this. "It's Sam Butler, my costar. I had no idea he was coming."

"Can't he get a hotel?"

"They're all booked," I reminded him.

"So he's staying with you?" Jackson repeated, as if clarifying he'd heard correctly.

I leaned back into my pillows and closed my eyes, feeling a headache coming on. "I hadn't planned on it. But I can't kick him to the curb."

"You don't think this is weird, Joey? I mean, we're official now. And another guy is staying at your place."

"It's weird. But he and I are just friends. There's nothing funny going on between us."

The sounds in the background faded, and I pictured Jackson moving away from the crowd. "I don't like this, Joey. I mean, I don't care what people think. You know that. But if the press finds you and sees this . . . if word gets out . . . there's going to be speculation. It's not a great way to start our future."

I understood what he was saying, but . . . "You trust me, don't you?"

"Of course I trust you. But . . ."

But what? Was there a condition on his trust? Was that what he meant?

"What do you want me to do?" I finally asked. "Kick him out?"

Jackson didn't say anything for a moment. "No, I know you don't want to do that. I guess I'll just have to deal."

Just have to deal?

This was not the way I wanted our relationship to go. First, I'd offended Jackson by asking if we could keep our relationship quiet. Now this.

I already felt like I was failing at the relationship thing, and more than anything I wanted it to succeed. Then again, maybe it was like I had thought earlier. Maybe finding Desiree in my house had set off some kind of bad luck chain reaction.

I had to find out what happened to her before this streak continued—especially now that it seemed like Jackson had been added to the mix. We should be the happiest we've ever been, and instead all I felt was the weight of tension.

"I love you, Jackson." My voice cracked as I said the words.

"I love you too."

But as I ended the call, everything felt wrong. I walked to the window and slid it open, trying to let some air in. Instead, sounds of another fight next door assaulted my ears.

I just needed to go to sleep. Now.

Because this day hadn't gone anything like I'd wanted it to.

CHAPTER
ELEVEN

WHILE SAM SLEPT on the couch, I quietly slipped out of the house to meet my friend Phoebe for an early morning smoothie and a heart-to-heart talk.

I hadn't gotten a wink of sleep last night.

For starters, I hadn't gone to bed when I'd said I was going to bed. No, I'd sat out in the living room catching up with Sam.

Then when I'd tried again to go to sleep, I'd kept hearing creaks come from above me. Yeah, that's right. In the room where Desiree died. I imagined her walking around up there. Asking for help. Declaring that she was going to be someone. Desperate for a role in my TV show.

I imagined her angry. Angry at me for not being here. For not interceding.

I had to get a grip. I didn't believe in ghosts. Then why had I felt so terrified?

Rest became a distant reality.

So then I'd gotten up and studied my script.

But, of course, I hadn't been able to actually study my script. Because I started thinking about Jackson. I kept thinking about the hurt look on his face when I'd asked to keep our relationship quiet. I thought about the disappointment in his voice when I'd told him about Sam being here.

For a moment—and just a moment—everything had felt blissful. It had gone downhill very fast. And now I felt like I was questioning everything.

More than anything, I wanted to be with Jackson. But how would our lives blend? How would we make it work when so many in Hollywood came from a string of broken relationships? I already had the start of that string. I was divorced after a horrible marriage.

I didn't want that to ever happen again.

Then again, who did? What would set me apart from everyone else who'd been in my shoes before?

Finally, I'd decided to take a shower and get ready. Phoebe needed to get to Oh Buoy, a smoothie shack, at six a.m. to start her shift. I was meeting her at 5:30 to talk first. I'd texted her after midnight and she must have sensed my desperation because she said yes. I was eternally grateful.

It was still dark as I stepped outside. At least everything was quiet at my neighbors' house.

Ten minutes later, I pulled up to Oh Buoy. The small restaurant was located across the street from the beach and had a mix of nautical and tiki bar decorations. It was one of my favorite hangouts.

I knocked at the glass door. Phoebe appeared from the back and let me inside. My friend was one of these all-natural beauties who didn't have to wear makeup, fix her hair, or even wear nice clothes, and she still looked like a million bucks. Most people would call my fit, blonde friend a beach bunny, and I supposed she was. But she was a humble beach bunny with a wholesome smile and generous spirit. She was quiet, didn't like attention, and she was a hard worker.

She was basically my opposite.

Oh, and her sister had been married to Jackson. But she'd died of cancer.

"Morning, Joey." Phoebe locked the door behind me before offering a quick hug. It had been two weeks since we'd seen each other. "I came in extra early to get things ready. I figured that way we could talk without interruption."

"You're the best," I told her.

She was.

"And I made your favorite smoothie," she said. "It's in the booth over there. Let's sit and enjoy the quiet before chaos breaks out later. This time of year is so busy."

"You don't even know how much I need this. Thank you." I took a sip of my Mirlo Sunrise, and delight danced over my taste buds at the icy, citrusy flavor.

"You look tired."

"I couldn't sleep last night."

Phoebe leaned forward, her smoothie between her hands but untouched. "What's going on?"

So I told her about the dead body, about the fighting couple, about Sam showing up.

"Wow—that's a lot of stuff going on," she said. "Another average day in the life of Joey Darling."

"And there's Jackson. We had the conversation last night. You know, the one where we told each other we didn't want to date anyone else."

Her eyes widened. "That's awesome. But I figured it was coming."

I nodded. "I really love him, Phoebe."

"I'm so happy for you."

"Thanks." My voice lacked enthusiasm, but I took a long sip of my drink, hoping to conceal my inner turmoil. Yesterday had been a wonderful turning point in our relationship. It was just too bad we'd argued and disagreed so much afterward.

I frowned at the memory.

Phoebe studied my face. "Why do you look burdened?"

I sucked on my bottom lip for a moment, trying to decide how much to share. And then I decided not to hold back, and I did one of my conversation pukes all over her. "I think I offended Jackson because I asked if we could keep our relationship a secret. It isn't that I'm ashamed or that I don't want people to know. It's just that I don't want the *wrong* people to know. And then Sam showed up, and all the hotels in town were booked, and he just assumed he could stay with me, so he did. But Jackson didn't like that. And I can understand why. But I just feel that, as soon as Jackson and I got serious, everything has been going downhill."

I stopped and took a breath, waiting for Phoebe's reaction. She knew Jackson well—she was his sister-in-law, but the two were like brother and sister. They had a great relationship.

Her eyebrows knit together, and she nodded slowly as she processed. "Wow."

"That's all? Wow?" I had to admit that I was a little disappointed.

She shrugged. "I wouldn't stress too much about it. Jackson just doesn't like a lot of drama."

"But I'm an actress. Why would he want to be with me? I'm all about drama."

"That's not what I meant. I just mean he likes things simple—"

"Need I remind you how complicated my life is?" I resisted the urge to let my forehead hit the table in my normal dramatic fashion.

Phoebe frowned. "I'm sure it will all work out, Joey. Jackson wouldn't be with you if he didn't love you."

"How are our lives going to blend?" I continued. "I'll be away filming. He'll be here. What if I mess him up?"

"Mess him up? What are you talking about, Joey?" Phoebe tilted her head, looking honestly confused.

"I just mean that he has a good life. When I bring my craziness into it . . . it's not going to look the same."

"He's smart. I'm sure he's considered that. I can tell you're anxious."

"Anxious is an understatement." I squeezed my eyes shut. "Things have been relatively calm for the past four weeks since everything went down with my mom and dad. I guess I just hoped that would continue."

"Your life is about to change. You're going to film a TV show four hours from here. You bought a house. You're getting serious with Jackson. And then there's the dead body found at your house . . ."

"I know." My life *could* be a TV show.

She pressed her fingertips together in a yoga pose and straightened her back. "Just take a few deep breaths. Everything will be fine. And talk to Jackson about this. You two can figure this out."

"You're right. I'm overreacting. I think maybe the stress of all these changes is getting to me."

Just then, someone knocked at the door. It was time for Oh Buoy to open. Our conversation was done.

"Thanks for being a listening ear," I told Phoebe, grabbing my smoothie. "I appreciate it."

"Any time, Joey. Any time."

When I walked back out to my red Miata, I was surprised to see Jennifer standing beside it.

This was just great. Did I have someone else following me?

Seriously, when I encouraged people to "follow" me, I was just talking about on Instagram, not parking lots.

"Hi, Joey." Jennifer straightened and sniffled. Her eyes were red-rimmed still and her terse expression indicated she was still upset. Maybe even hysterical.

Hysterical people weren't my favorite to deal with.

"Hi there. It's early. And you're standing by my car." I paused in front of her—and therefore in front of my car.

"I'm sorry to insert myself into your day like this. But I really need to talk to you."

"Not the police?"

"I've heard you're actually a better detective than they are."

I might have beamed a little.

"Did you?" Then I realized the delusion I was living under and snapped out of it. "I'm actually not. I'm pretty terrible."

"But the police aren't going to get what I'm talking about. You will. You're an actress."

"What's going on, Jennifer?" The sun already beat down on me. It was going to be another hot July day. Not to mention that it was already getting busy. Three surfers had just walked past, boards in hand, and carloads of tourists headed toward the public parking access in the distance.

"I've been trying to call Desiree's boyfriend, Michael Mills. I haven't been able to get up with him, which is weird, you know? He's one of those people who's always attached to his phone."

That did sound strange. "You think he had something to do with this?"

She twirled her hands in the air, indicating her wheel of thought needed to keep going.

"Well, give me a minute to finish here. I finally called Michael's parents because I thought it was weird that he wasn't answering. I mean, he should be worried about Desiree. That's what I thought at first, at least. And then I realized I needed to tell him what happened." Her voice cracked.

"Go ahead."

She swallowed hard and her gaze caught mine. "His parents said that he's actually here in Nags Head."

I sucked in a quick breath. "What? Did he come with Desiree?"

"No. He didn't. She didn't tell me that, at least. And I talked to her the night before she died. She would have mentioned it."

"So you think Michael followed Desiree here." It was another puzzle piece. But did it fit?

"I think he did. And I have no idea why."

"Can we find him and ask him?" Maybe this was the lead we were looking for.

Jennifer frowned in a big, overblown expression. "That's the thing. His parents said he was in a car accident. He's at the hospital on a ventilator."

She let out a sob and fanned her face, her motions nearly manic.

"What?" That threw a wrench in things.

Jennifer nodded. "I started to go there, but I thought I should tell someone first."

"Did they say when this accident happened?"

"Apparently, it was the same night . . ."

" . . . that Desiree died." I finished.

"Exactly."

This Michael Mills guy was looking more and more suspicious all the time.

I nodded as I processed that. "This has been helpful, Jennifer. Thank you."

I passed her and walked toward the driver side door.

"What are you going to do?"

"I'm going to tell Jackson—I mean, Detective Sullivan."

CHAPTER
TWELVE

I COULDN'T GET up with Jackson—which bothered me. But maybe he was doing something all police-y, and he couldn't answer.

So I decided to go to the hospital myself.

If Michael Mills couldn't talk, I wasn't sure what I would prove by visiting him. But I was going to try anyway.

The woman at the front desk directed me to the second floor. I walked through the hospital corridor, my stomach churning at the scent of disinfectant. I didn't have good memories of hospitals. Not after I'd spent time in one after my ex had pushed me down the stairs.

Before I reached Michael Mills' room, I spotted a couple lingering outside his doorway. I slowed my steps and quickly soaked in their features. The woman appeared to be in her fifties with blonde hair that looked plastered in place. The man had ruddy skin and was probably thirty pounds overweight.

A bag sat on the floor beside them, along with three discarded coffee cups.

As the woman looked over at me, her eyes lit with recognition, as if she'd run into an old friend or something. "You're Joey Darling."

I braced myself for what was to come. I never knew where that starting line might lead. Despite my hesitation, I took three more steps until I stopped in front of them. "I am."

"I'm a huge fan," she gushed. "I absolutely adored *Family Secrets*, and I can't wait to buy it on DVD whenever it comes out."

"Thank you. I always like to hear that." I paused, examining the woman's red-rimmed eyes.

This had to be Michael's mother and father. That made sense. And—I glanced at the number on the door—this was definitely his room.

"Are you here to see . . . Michael?" The man examined my face. Was he looking for grief? For some type of signal as to why I'd shown up?

"Yes."

"You know Michael?" the woman said. "You must have met him through Desiree."

I wasn't following her train of thought. "You think I met Michael through Desiree?"

She let out an uncertain, quick fading chuckle. "Well, yes, since Desiree got a role on your show and everything. She was so excited about it and talked like it might be her big break."

Oh boy.

Change the subject. Detecting 101. Sometimes it was just best to avoid answering. "How is Michael?"

"There haven't been any changes." His dad frowned, and his voice turned solemn. "But the doctor expects a full recovery."

"That's good news. I wasn't sure exactly what happened. Did I hear correctly that he was in a car accident?"

Michael's mom shook her head, her eyes welling with moisture again. "That's right. Apparently, he was turning onto the street when another car T-boned him. I just can't believe it."

"That's awful," I said. And it was. A friend of mine had been in a horrible car accident three years ago, and she now lived with chronic pain. "Did the police catch the person responsible?"

"No, not yet. That's what they told us, at least. It was a hit-and-run." His mom sniffled.

"I'm so sorry."

"I hope the police find the person responsible for this . . . and make him pay." Mr. Mills' voice went from solemn to angry, and his expression matched.

I couldn't blame him. "People should take responsibility for their actions."

Mrs. Mills shifted and looked beyond me, as if she'd taken a mental shift. "Speaking of which, I can't believe Desiree hasn't come by yet."

I sucked in a deep breath. They didn't know about Desiree, I realized.

Did that mean I had to be the one to break it to them?

Dread pooled in my stomach. I should have never come here without Jackson.

Jackson still wasn't answering his phone, and a less secure woman might have tried to track him down. Okay, I'd considered it. Maybe I'd even driven past the police station to see if his car was there. It wasn't.

So I'd gone back to the house to process what I'd just learned.

When I walked inside, Sam was in the kitchen cooking something that smelled delicious. Fat particles floated in the air and teased like the Pied Piper leading me toward Fat Camp.

"Good morning." He put another piece of bacon in a sizzling skillet. "I ran to the store and picked up some groceries. Decided to make a late breakfast. I fixed enough for you."

"That's really nice of you. Thank you." I slid into a seat at the bar so I could watch. "How did you sleep last night?"

"Like a baby—thanks to my sleeping meds. Never leave home without them."

My old life kept flashing back to me over and over again. Self-medicating instead of dealing with issues. Drinking instead of facing reality. Staying busy instead of admitting emptiness. I hadn't realized I'd done any of those things until I'd come here and seen what my life could look like away from the limelight.

"I see," I said.

Sam placed a plate in front of me. "Enjoy. Or *bon appetit*, as they say."

"I never knew you liked to cook." I picked up my fork.

"A lot has changed in my life over the past year or so." He stood across from me to eat his eggs benedict.

"Is that right? Like what?" He hadn't shared anything last night.

He offered a half shrug—a motion that appeared to take way too much effort. "You don't want to hear all of my sad tales."

"I'm always happy to listen, Sam."

"Kelsey left me." His voice cracked.

I sat up straight. "What? Last night you said she was great."

"I lied. She dumped me for Colin Moore."

My bottom lip dropped open. "Colin Moore? You're way more handsome than he is."

"Thanks. She doesn't think so, however."

My eyes widened. I hadn't expected that. My bacon suddenly didn't taste as good. "I had no idea. I'm so sorry, Sam."

"Don't be sorry. One day I woke up and realized I had to make the best of my life. I learned to cook. I took art classes. I started doing yoga on the beach . . . with goats."

"Wow. On all counts—including the goats."

"Yes, wow. I got myself back together. And then I got the call about *Relentless*. Perfect timing, huh?" He bit into a piece of crispy bacon and then pointed with it to emphasize his words.

"It sounds like it."

We continued to chat as we ate breakfast. It was good to talk to Sam, to catch up with an old friend, even if all his news wasn't good. At least I could be a listening ear for him.

After Sam and I cleaned up, we started to rehearse the lines for the premiere episode of the new season. We stood in the kitchen, scripts in hand, and read through the scenes together. I figured it was a good use of time until I could get up with Jackson. And this helped me not think about Desiree and her dead body upstairs and the total and complete lack of answers I had concerning my non-investigation into her death.

"I don't feel like I'm connecting with this scene." Sam pointed to the script. "I need to go deeper if I'm going to sell this. What do you think? Should it sound more certain or more like a surprise?"

The scene we were going over involved Raven and Grant—played by Sam—being stuck in an old underground room and trying to get out, to no avail. When they think they're going to die down there, Grant decides to confess his love. True love this time because they'd already kissed before. Of course, things were never as simple as they seemed. Especially when Grant's wife returns from the dead later in the season.

I stared at his lines of dialogue, trying to interpret them. "I definitely think you should sound certain. You're declaring your love."

"But I'm also scared because I could jeopardize the friendship." He scrunched his face in uncertainty.

He had a point. And everyone thought acting was so easy. In reality, it was emotionally exhausting.

"Okay, so you have to add a little more depth to it." I closed my eyes so I could picture the scene playing out.

Playing Raven Remington came back to me as easily as riding a bike.

"So I'll step closer," Sam said.

"Maybe brush my hair out of my eyes," I suggested. "That's always a sweet gesture."

"Like this?" He pushed my hair back.

"Yes, exactly like that. And then tell me how you feel." I waited, listening for Sam to sell it.

"I love you. I always have. I always will." His voice cracked with emotion.

That wasn't too bad. I almost believed it.

And now it was my turn.

I stepped closer to him and raised my head.

"I love you too. I was wondering when you would tell me." My voice sounded wispy with fake emotions.

"Joey?"

Startled, I jumped back. My real name was not supposed to be muttered in this scene.

I turned and saw Jackson standing at the door, staring at us.

I knew beyond a doubt that things weren't going to get any easier between us today.

CHAPTER
THIRTEEN

"WHAT IS GOING ON HERE?" Jackson stood with his hands on his hips, his gaze burning into me.

I must have left the door cracked—at the most inconvenient of times, of course. Just like in those stupid movies.

I rushed toward him, realizing how that might have looked and sounded. I stopped just short of touching Jackson. Yet, even then, I could feel the steam coming from him.

"We're just rehearsing," I explained.

"That's not what it looked like." Jackson glowered at Sam, who raised his hands in the air in surrender.

"Totally just rehearsing," Sam said, keeping his distance like any smart man would do right now. "You must be Joey's fresh catch."

I swerved my head toward Sam, horrified at his word choice. *Fresh catch*? Had he lost his mind? So much for thinking of him as a smart man.

I couldn't deal with that right now. "Sam, this is Jackson Sullivan. My boyfriend."

Sam's eyebrows shot up. "Seriously? I had no idea. All that catching up we did last night, and you didn't mention that, Joey? Congratulations."

I was seriously going to kill Sam. But I'd save that for later. Instead, through clenched teeth, I said, "Jackson, this is Sam Butler, my *Relentless* costar."

Jackson still looked steamed as he nodded at Sam. "Can I have a word with you, Joey? Privately?"

I felt like I was being called into the principal's office, but I nodded and followed Jackson outside to my deck. Dread seized all my muscles until I felt stiff all over as we stood in front of each other.

"What is going on?" Jackson crossed his arms, keeping his distance from me.

"We were just rehearsing. I promise. I know it must have looked funny—"

"It looked like you were about to kiss."

I opened my mouth and shut it again as I considered my words. "I wasn't going to kiss Sam *here*."

"What does that mean?" Jackson's voice rose with frustration.

That hadn't come out right, had it? "You do realize that I'll have to kiss Sam when I'm on the set, right? But only there. And only as a part of playing my character."

His jaw flexed. Jackson still wasn't happy, and I wasn't sure how to make things better. People in the real world didn't have these conversations. People in real life didn't get paid to pretend they loved someone else while the whole thing was being filmed.

Now that I said it that way, it did seem a little sordid, didn't it?

"Jackson . . ." I reached for him, but he stiffened. Instead, I dropped my hand to the side. "Onscreen kisses aren't like real kisses. They're technical, and they make me self-conscious and . . . you'd be surprised how many actors have horrible breath."

He didn't even react to the breath comment. That wasn't a good sign.

"I just need a minute." He ran a hand over his face. Turned away. Let out a sigh.

Why did I feel like everything was slipping away? Why couldn't just one thing in my life work like I wanted? Panic started to boil inside me.

"I know I've already said this, but I think it bears repeating," Jackson finally said, his words slow and purposeful. "I don't think your friend should stay here with you, Joey."

"And, like I've already asked, where is Sam supposed to stay? Everything in town is booked. This is one of the most popular weeks of the summer, and there are no vacancies in town. We've talked about this."

"Can't he go back to wherever he came from?" The words sounded harsh, though I wasn't sure if Jackson intended them that way. Maybe he had.

"He came here so we could rehearse."

Jackson's gaze darkened, and he still looked both uneasy and unhappy. "I'm not loving these rehearsals."

"And his girlfriend left him. When Eric and I had problems, Sam was there for me."

"That's nice of him, but this . . . this is different."

"Different or not, you trust me, right?" The question hung in the air. I needed Jackson to say yes. I needed him to be on my side. I needed him to be the Harry to my Sally.

I waited for his answer, hardly able to breathe. I felt like my future hung in the balance, and the scale wasn't tilting in my favor.

"This isn't about me trusting you or not." Jackson's words sounded stiff with self-control. "I'm just asking that you respect me enough to not let him stay here."

"And I'm just asking that you trust me." Was I being stubborn? I didn't know. But I didn't think it was fair that Jackson was asking me to rearrange things because he was feeling territorial.

We stared at each other, and I felt something beginning to shift between us.

I hated it. I wanted to make things right. I wanted to rewind this conversation.

Yet I couldn't bring myself to apologize.

My heart pounded as I waited for whatever would happen next.

"I guess I know where I stand then." Jackson shook his head and turned to walk away. "I need to get back to work."

"Why'd you stop by?"

"It's not important," he muttered.

I knew I should call after him. But calling after him would mean I'd be the one compromising.

Maybe that was what I *should* do. Maybe it was the right thing. The mature thing.

But thoughts of my first marriage pummeled me. I remembered the mess it had been. How it had started with so much warmth and fun and turned into a total disaster when I'd realized that Eric was insecure and possessive.

Was that what was happening with Jackson also?

The thought of it broke my heart.

I didn't go back inside after Jackson left. I stood on my deck, despite the heat and humidity. There wasn't even a breeze today to offer me any relief. No, instead a fly annoyed me and a lifeguard in the distance repeatedly blew his whistle.

I didn't want to face Sam and explain myself or act as if nothing had happened—although he had stuck his head out the door and told me he was going to shower and lay down for a few minutes. The man could be so clueless sometimes, but that worked to my advantage right now. I didn't want to talk.

As I stood outside, I felt a little dead inside. Like I'd been named prom queen only to have pig's blood poured over me.

Okay, maybe not quite that Stephen King dramatic.

This wasn't like Jackson and me. We didn't fight like this. He understood my idiosyncrasies, and they amused him. I understood his toughness, and I reveled in it. Our opposing personalities actually brought us closer—until now.

Now . . . I didn't know what I was feeling, except for confused. All the fears that I buried deep inside wanted to boil to the surface.

"Hey, Joey." Zane stepped onto the deck.

I hadn't even heard him pull up or climb the stairs. I was totally and completely wrapped up in my own thoughts, wasn't I?

I wiped my tears away and straightened, unwilling to show him how upset I was. I was smart enough to know that crying on Zane's shoulder would be a bad, bad idea.

"Hey, Zane." I pulled myself together. "What brings you by here?"

"I was hoping I might catch Jackson—or you. You'll do also."

"Okay . . ." I was Zane's second choice, which was kind of weird considering Zane and Jackson's history. "What's going on?"

He stood beside me at the railing. "First, are you okay?"

He'd noticed I was upset. Of course. The problem with Zane and me was that we were too much alike. He was intuitive and could sense when to move in. Wait, did I say move in? I meant he could sense when I was having a bad day.

"Just a little argument with Jackson," I finally said.

He offered a half-frown as he glanced at me. "I'm sorry. You want to talk about it?"

"Not really." What I wanted to do was erase it. Was that possible?

Zane shifted toward me. "I'll get to the point of why I'm here. Wesley called me again. It was about that painting he thought he left under the bed."

I glanced at Zane, wondering where he was going with this. "Okay."

"Apparently, it was valuable. Hashtag: worthafortune!"

"Then why did he leave it?" People generally grabbed the expensive stuff first—not as an afterthought. I waited to hear his explanation.

"I don't know. I think Wesley forgot he put it under the bed. He said he didn't usually use that room except for overflow storage. It wasn't until later that he realized it was missing."

"Why did he put the painting under the bed?" I mean, I could understand if it was several paintings he'd placed there. But just one? It seemed weird.

Zane shrugged, his curly hair bouncing in the breeze. "Again—for storage. His closets were full. His walls were lined. He was running out of room. Someone at an online gallery that carries his work just contacted him about it, offering to pay one hundred thousand for this particular piece."

My eyebrows shot up. "Not a bad paycheck."

"Not bad at all. Except Wesley can't find it." Zane's eyes scrunched together, like he was preparing himself for my reaction.

"You mean that, after all of that, the painting wasn't under the bed?" I couldn't even remember what had happened after I'd found the dead body. I'd completely forgotten about the artwork we'd originally gone to fetch, and it hadn't seemed important enough to ask about then.

"I mean, I don't know," Zane said. "I never looked."

"You're right. Everything is a blur after we found Desiree dead."

Zane nodded toward the house behind me, his eyes lit with hopefulness. "Can I go look for it?"

"I'm not supposed to go upstairs. And, if the artwork was there, I'm sure the police took it for evidence." I straightened as an idea hit me. "Zane, what if that's what this crime is about—that painting? What if Desiree tried to steal it?"

Why hadn't I thought about that earlier?

Zane twisted his head in confusion. "I thought Desiree came here to find you?"

My thoughts raced ahead of me. "Maybe she did. But maybe she somehow stumbled onto this in the process. I mean, I heard she didn't have a job and was desperate for money. Desiree could have found that painting and figured she had a way out."

Zane let out an uncertain-sounding sigh. "How would she know it was valuable? And that would mean she sneaked inside your house. There was no sign of that, right?"

"I wouldn't put it past her. My neighbor said he saw her sitting on the deck, apparently waiting for me to get here. What if she decided to wait inside? She probably didn't have money for a hotel room. Not according to what I've heard."

Zane nodded slowly. "You could be on to something here. Let's keep talking."

The scene played out in my head. "So she sneaks inside the house. I didn't see any signs of forced entry—"

"But there was a realtor lock box. There's a chance she could have figured out the code and gotten that key. It takes time, but it's entirely possible. There are only ten thousand different combinations of numbers, and if someone has time to go through them . . ."

"So she does that. Goes inside. Sees the place is empty. She knows I'm moving in here because it was in the tabloids." I frowned as those last words left my lips.

"I saw that. Someone must have seen you during a walk-through last week and snapped a picture." Zane shrugged almost apologetically.

I released a sigh, not surprised. "Anyway, it doesn't matter now. Desiree comes here, waits for me, decides to go inside. Then she goes upstairs— maybe she's just being nosy. And she finds that painting. How hard would it have been for her to look up the previous owner of the house? She could have seen his name and looked up his work."

"It's a possibility," Zane said. "Wesley does have a web presence."

My heart skipped a beat as my mental movie kept

playing. I felt like we were finally onto something. "Maybe she started to leave with the painting when someone walked in on her."

Zane crossed his arms and shifted until his hip rested against the deck rail. With the sand dune behind him and the bright sun shining overhead, he could be a poster boy for beach living.

"Who would have walked in on her?" Zane asked. "The house was under contract—no other realtors should have been showing it."

There was only one person who made sense. "Wesley."

Zane's eyes widened, and he straightened with shock, as if I'd told him *Star Wars* was a disgrace to modern movies or something. "Wesley? No. He's a lover not a fighter. An artist, not a savage."

"If someone tried to steal his work, I'd bet he'd fight."

Zane shook his head, as if he felt a headache coming on. "But if Wesley was in town on the day Desiree died, why wouldn't he have come to the closing? He canceled at the last minute."

"Maybe he wanted to prove he wasn't in town so he wouldn't look guilty." It sounded smart to me.

Zane and I both stood there in silence. This sounded like the most plausible theory yet.

Though part of me wanted to stay out of this investigation, another part of me wanted answers. I wanted to be able to enjoy my house until I had to leave to begin filming. Was that too much to ask? I didn't know. I just knew that I wouldn't be getting any true rest under this roof until I knew what had happened to Desiree.

"Do you know of any art galleries in town that carry Wesley's work?" I asked, feeling like I'd found my first decent lead.

"I know of one."

"I want to go there. Now." Maybe this would keep my mind off Jackson. And if I found Desiree's killer, maybe my string of bad luck would end.

Maybe.

CHAPTER
FOURTEEN

OUTER BANKS ART galleries weren't like NYC galleries.

I'd always wanted to be a connoisseur of art and culture, but in truth I was a girl from the Virginia mountains who'd grown up with nothing. Hollywood had changed me, but, as the saying went, you could take a girl out of the country but you couldn't take the country out of the girl.

The Sea Glass House, as it was called, was a converted beach home. It had a quirky feel with squeaky wooden floors, and it smelled strongly of essential oils. Clove, maybe? I was no expert.

Each room had a different theme. There was the driftwood art theme. Sea glass art theme. And then there was the room with Wesley's paintings. I soaked in his artwork for a moment. He seemed to specialize in landscape portraits of the beach, but he'd added a unique twist by using bright colors and almost cartoon-like graphics. It was a modern take on a classic oil painting.

Were these sophisticated? I wouldn't think so.

But they had a pop culture art appeal. To me, at least. I liked them.

"It's like Bob Ross," Zane whispered. "Everything is happy. Hashtag: Bobwouldbeproud."

Zane was a huge Bob Ross fan. In fact, we used to like watching reruns of the show together, usually while eating hummus and drinking smoothies. Those were fun days, but I knew I had to leave them behind, especially when I considered my history with Zane.

"I agree. I think Bob Ross would approve."

"Can I help you?" a man asked behind me.

I turned and saw a prim and proper gentleman with a thin, neat goatee and mustache. His name tag read, "Art," which I found entirely appropriate.

"I like these." I nodded toward Wesley's paintings. "Is the artist local?"

"He just moved from the Outer Banks." Art practically glowed as he talked about Wesley's work. "But his paintings are wonderful, aren't they? He's one of our most popular artists, and his work is finally getting the recognition it deserves."

"The cost seems reasonable." Most were priced below five hundred dollars.

Art raised his chin. "I'll give you an inside tip here. These paintings will be increasing in value soon, so I'd buy now while you can."

That was interesting . . . "Why are they going up in value?"

Art looked around before leaning closer. "Of course, art is only worth what someone is willing to pay for it. Let's just say that people have been willing to pay quite a lot for Wesley's work recently."

"That's happy little news for him, I guess." Zane nodded as he said the words, looking entirely too pleased with himself for tapping in to his inner Bob Ross.

Art squinted as he studied my face. "You're that actress, aren't you?"

"That's right. Joey Darling." As I said the words, I couldn't help but think about how Jackson probably wouldn't approve of me doing this. He liked me to keep out of trouble, and I seemed to gravitate toward it. But asking questions never hurt anyone, right?

I knew from personal experience that wasn't exactly true. And the thought of Jackson caused another surge of sadness in me. I didn't want to fight with him. I didn't want to be stubborn, but I didn't want to be a pushover either. Perhaps finding the balance I needed was more challenging than I thought.

Art shifted, his mental gears obviously still turning. "Didn't you buy Wesley's house?"

"I did. How'd you know?" This man didn't strike me as a tabloid reader.

"He told me."

I suppose that made sense. "Is that right? I thought it would be nice to have some of his artwork in the house—but I wanted to check it out first, you know?"

"Of course."

"Every house tells a story. I want to preserve the history of this place—even its modern history—and I thought one of these paintings would do the trick. It would leave Mr. Twigg's footprint on the house."

The man's eyes lit, as if he'd realized that I was in a position to actually be able to afford something here. "I agree. That's a lovely idea."

I paused by one particular painting—one of the local lighthouses. I really did like it. "But I like to have my artwork signed."

"Mr. Twigg doesn't believe in signing his artwork on the front. He said it ruins the painting."

"But I'll only buy artwork if it's signed."

"I understand, but—"

"Any idea when Wesley might be back in town? I

really want to ask him myself if he'll sign his artwork for me. It's most definitely a deal breaker."

Art looked around again, as if there might be someone else inside the empty gallery. There wasn't. "He's still in town."

"Is that right? I had no idea. Is he in hiding?" I laughed like the idea was funny. In truth, I laughed to cover my suspicion that Wesley was hiding because he was guilty.

"He's trying to finish one more piece before he leaves. He's strange like that. Once he starts something, he likes to complete it. Moving locations might mess with his mojo, he feared."

"Understandable." I knew all about the creative life—the good, the bad, and the ugly of it. "Any idea where he's staying? I'd like to meet him."

"My understanding is that he's staying with a friend."

"You know this friend's name or how to find him?"

"Well, I couldn't possibly tell you that." Art shrugged, like he was above it and slightly offended that I'd asked.

"There's no way I can track him down then?" I continued.

"That would be highly unprofessional. But I'd be happy to call him for you."

"I'd really like to talk to him myself," I pressed.

"Maybe I could arrange that—after I call him."

I plastered on another grin. "You see, this is part of my problem. I like immediate results. I know it's a character flaw. I really do. But I'd like to talk to him today."

Art glanced at his watch. "I have a tour group coming in thirty minutes, and I've got to get ready for them. But I'd be happy to contact him afterward."

"I suppose that will work. I just hope I don't change my mind during the time in between."

"She can be fickle like that," Zane added.

I turned to walk away, hoping my ploy paid off. I think I might have come on too strong. Maybe I should have let it play out more. But it was too late for that.

Zane followed me toward the door, flashing a peace sign to Art.

"Wait!" Art called.

I paused and held my breath, waiting to hear what he said.

"I can't tell you an address, but I can say that he's staying with someone named Dizzy."

My mouth dropped open.

Dizzy?

What? How had I missed this?

"So Wesley *is* in town. But he doesn't want anyone to know. Why?" I asked, once I was back in my car with Zane beside me. I cranked the AC, but the humidity was still winning. The day was getting hotter and hotter as it went on.

"There's only one reason I can think of. He's guilty." Zane sounded disappointed. He must have really liked Wesley. Then again, Zane could get along with anybody. He was Mr. Social, which was what made him a good real estate agent.

"Exactly!" My voice rose a little too much in excitement. But Zane and I were on the same page, and it felt good to have someone actually agree with me.

"He must have planned that whole being out of town for closing thing so he could cover his tracks."

I glanced at Zane. "But Dizzy?"

I still couldn't figure out how she fit into this.

"I'm surprised she didn't tell you about her new roommate," Zane said.

"*I'm* surprised she didn't tell me. I mean, this is Dizzy. I just saw her yesterday." Dizzy was an over-sharer. This just didn't make sense.

"Maybe we should go pay her a visit," Zane suggested.

"Oh, we should definitely go pay her a visit." I put the car in reverse and started toward Beach Combers.

Ten minutes later, we pulled up to a pink-sided house that had been converted into a hair salon. I stared at the place for a moment. This was where I'd gotten my start when I'd moved here. I'd been broke, with no acting jobs on the horizon and a deep-seated desire to locate my father, whom I hadn't heard from in months. I'd gone back to my roots—actual roots, not hair color roots. I'd started working for my aunt, and Jackson had been one of my first customers.

At the thought of Jackson, my heart sagged.

Where was he right now? What was he thinking? Was the end of Jacksoey? Or was it Joeyson? Either way . . .

I couldn't even think about that right now.

And maybe that was why I was jumping into this investigation with both feet. It was distracting me from other issues at hand.

Like the fact that Sam Butler was waiting back at my house.

More guilt pressed in on me.

"You sure you're okay?" Zane asked as we sat there in my car, neither getting out.

I nodded, though my heart felt heavy. "Yeah, I guess my fight with Jackson is bothering me more than I thought. I can't stop thinking about it."

"I'm sorry to hear that."

"Me too. But that's real life, right?"

"Every couple I know has disagreements. Unless

one is just a real pushover, I guess. And neither you nor Jackson are pushovers."

Nope, Jackson and I both had strong feelings on things. I hoped that would work in harmony together.

"I wouldn't worry about it, Joey," Zane said. "He'll come around. He's obviously crazy about you."

"If he doesn't?" My throat ached as the words left my mouth.

Because I knew this was bigger than one disagreement. I knew I'd be leaving soon, and then Jackson and I wouldn't see each other as much. I knew that things were going to change, and that scared the dickens out of me.

"You'll always have me waiting in the wings." Zane flashed a smile.

I let out a terse laugh. "Very funny."

I actually didn't know if Zane was joking or not. But I was going to assume that he was.

"We should probably go talk to Dizzy now," I said, my hand on the door handle.

"Yeah, probably."

CHAPTER
FIFTEEN

"JOEY! Zane! What brings the two of you here?" Dizzy paused as she rolled an older woman's hair in curlers. "Jingle Bells" played on the overhead.

Every day was a good day for Christmas music, as far as Dizzy was concerned. Even in July. I was surprised she hadn't put up a tree yet or donned a Santa hat.

"Did you decide you wanted to work here again and forget about that whole *Relentless* show and being famous?" Dizzy continued.

"Not exactly." I paused and the scent of perm solution and hair spray hit me.

Part of me missed this old place. It wasn't that I wanted to work here again, but it did hold some memories. Memories of simpler moments. Memories of when life felt normal and ordinary for a blip in time.

There was a lot to be said for that. I'd pulled myself back together here. I'd rediscovered the person I was before I became famous.

I turned back to Dizzy. "I actually have a couple questions for you."

"Can you ask now? Or do you need privacy?"

I glanced at the elderly woman whose hair Dizzy was fixing. She tried to look uninterested, but her eyes kept darting toward me in the mirror. She was definitely listening.

"Privacy would be great," I said.

"Let me put two more rollers in, and I'm all yours. For a few minutes at least."

Five minutes later, we were in the back room of the hair salon. Dizzy moved some magazines, as well as boxes full of products, off the table and motioned we could sit there. I decided to stand instead.

"So what's going on?" Dizzy's eyes danced with curiosity.

"Do you have someone living with you, Dizzy?" I got right to the point.

Her curious eyes grew wide. "Living with me?"

"Yes, like, at your house," I clarified.

Realization rolled over her features . . . along with a touch of what appeared to be guilt. "Well . . . kind of. 'Living with me' seems like a strong way to word it."

"What does that mean?"

She frowned, almost comically. "It means that I took in a boarder."

I was hoping this was all a mistake. Obviously, it wasn't. "You didn't tell me that. Are you having financial trouble? Do you need help? You could have come to me."

Dizzy waved her hand in the air like she didn't have a care in the world. "No, no, no. It's not like that. I just saw the opportunity to make a little extra money, so I put it out there that I had a room to rent."

"And who's now living in that room?" I waited for her to admit the truth.

"His name is Wesley. He's in his fifties. I think you'd really like him."

"When did he move in?" She still hadn't admitted the man's connection to me. Was she clueless? Or was she trying to hide something?

"One week ago. But he's only staying for the summer, and then he's moving on."

I couldn't read Dizzy's expression, but she definitely didn't appear to feel guilty. That left me with the conclusion that she was somehow clueless about these details. "Is this Wesley a painter?"

"Yes, he is. How did you know?"

"Because I just bought his house!" My words came out a little louder than I intended.

Dizzy gasped and put a hand over her heart. "What?"

"He told everyone he'd moved up to Norfolk," Zane added.

"Well, obviously he hasn't. He's staying with me. Why would he move from that big, beautiful house to mine?" She pressed her lips together in confusion.

"That's what we'd like to know. We'd also like to know why he lied about being out of town." Wesley was looking guiltier by the moment. Had he chosen Dizzy on purpose? Did he know about our connection? And did he plan on using it for some type of ulterior purpose?

"He seems like a nice man," Dizzy said halfheartedly. "I'm sure it's all a coincidence."

"But he's hiding something," I told her. "Do you know if he's at your house now?"

"He's there almost all the time. I'd guess he's probably home at the moment. Not that he has to check in with me or something. I mean, it's strictly a professional thing that he's staying at my place. But the man is fascinating, especially when he has that magical paintbrush in his hands." She growled like a tiger.

And that was an image I would never be able to wash from my mind.

I leveled my gaze with hers. "I need to talk to him, Dizzy."

"Well, I'm certainly not going to stop you. But Mrs. Murphy's perm might."

———

It took only five minutes to get to Dizzy's place. She lived in a small house on the other side of the island, in a neighborhood filled with mostly full-timers. I was always amazed at how normal these neighborhoods felt, especially since the area in general was saturated with stilted vacation rentals. This neighborhood, on the other hand, had swing sets and flowerbeds.

Dizzy had given me a key, so I let myself in. She stayed in a bedroom on the bottom floor, but her boarder was staying upstairs in the room over the garage, apparently.

I wasted no time climbing the carpeted steps and pounding on the door. Zane hovered behind me, perfectly content to let me take the lead. A moment later, Wesley appeared.

He was in his fifties and looked fit. Though he had some gray at his temples, his hair was otherwise thick and dark. He wore a white apron with paint stains on it and, when I peered beyond him, I spotted an easel and the start of a painting.

His eyes widened when he saw me. "Joey Darling."

"You know me?" I already knew he did, but I wanted to hear what he had to say.

"You bought my house."

"Hi, Wesley," Zane called from behind me.

"Hello, Zane. Good to see you again." Wesley let out a feeble wave, followed by an equally as feeble laugh. "Can I help you both?"

"We thought you left town," I started. My tone sounded more accusatory than it should. But I was tired of people playing games. I wanted answers, and my creativity for ascertaining information had waned.

"My muse was here. I had to stay while she lingered and until I completed my latest painting." He shrugged, like that was normal. Something that sounded vaguely like an Italian accent crept in as he said the words. I halfway expected him to dramatically kiss the air while rolling his wrist with flair.

"Then why did you say you were out of town?" I continued. I couldn't care less if he was in town. I only cared because he was being deceitful.

"I just don't like to be bothered with things like meeting with lawyers."

Just as quickly as his accent appeared, it disappeared, leading me to believe that Wesley had created it to go along with some type of eccentric artist persona. Like I said earlier, I understood the creative life—the good, the bad, and the ugly of it. While my comrades in arms always kept me entertained, sometimes they also made me roll my eyes. I'm sure people probably said the same for me and my theatrics.

"I already went over the paperwork beforehand, and I knew everything was good," Wesley continued.

I crossed my arms, not so quick to believe his excuse—or his accent. "Is that the only reason?"

Wesley swallowed hard. "Of course. What else would it be?"

"Tell me about the painting you left at the house." I tried to sound all Raven Remington tough. I might as well use my acting skills to get me ahead in life, whether on the Big Screen or just finding answers and helping humanity.

"It was one of my favorites." Wesley's voice sounded wistful. "Beautiful, really. It was a seagull on a piling that I painted, but I broke it up until it looked like a mosaic."

"Then why did you leave it behind if it was one of your favorites?" Something wasn't adding up about his story.

"I didn't mean to. I hid it under that bed. Then I forgot I hid it there. I was preoccupied with another painting at the time and then I realized I should have waited to put my house on the market because I needed to stay in the area longer to finish this master-piece and I had to find somewhere to stay in the meantime because the process had already been started but I didn't want my fans to know I was still here because then they might track me down and . . ." He continued, barely taking a breath.

I still didn't buy it—the part I'd been able to keep up with, at least. "Wesley, are you saying that you didn't go back to the house to retrieve the painting? Are you saying you didn't kill Desiree?"

His eyes widened, and his voice rose. "Kill? Why would I kill someone?"

"That's what we need to know."

He raised his hands. "Look, I know this might sound suspicious. I did want that painting back. I *need* it back. Truth is, I didn't think it was all that special. But a picture of it was posted on an online auction, along with several of my other paintings. There was a bidding war for it, and someone wants to pay a hundred thousand dollars."

"That's a lot of money," Zane said.

"I know. I've never been offered that amount before, and I could really use the cash."

I wasn't ready to buy this guy's story yet. "Enough to kill for?"

"No! Of course not. But I'm about to have open heart surgery, and I could really use the paycheck. I don't have great insurance. I'm self-employed. I need that money."

Okay, *that* I might buy.

"And you have no idea where the painting is?" I clarified.

"I have no idea. But I need it. Desperately. Selling it is my chance to take my career to the next level. Don't get me wrong—I'm doing okay now. But this is the opportunity of a lifetime."

CHAPTER
SIXTEEN

BACK IN MY CAR, Zane and I looked at each other. No words were needed.

But we were going to exchange them anyway.

But this was only after we'd stopped by Sunrise Coffee Co., and I'd gotten some brain fuel. My new expression was "Drinking and Thinking." As long as that drinking only involved coffee, I was golden.

"Wesley didn't do this," Zane said.

Just as I said, "He's totally guilty."

Okay, so maybe words *were* needed.

I shifted toward Zane in my tiny yet impractical seat. "Why do you say that?"

"There's nothing that proves he has a connection to the victim." Zane's voice held an unwavering confidence that I didn't often hear in my free-spirited surfing friend who, at times, talked like a male version of a Valley Girl.

"But if Wesley came back for the painting and found Desiree with it, then he'd have a reason."

"But he would have gotten the painting and gotten out of town once he had it in his hands. Forget his muse."

I leaned back and took a sip of my coffee. Zane had a point. "This is so complicated."

"I agree." He glanced over at me. "What now?"

That was a great question. "I have no idea. I just need to think. If it wasn't Wesley, then I have no idea who it was. I'm not sure if we should examine him more or move on."

"Yet there's no one to move on to."

"Exactly! Except maybe Michael Mills—but he's on a ventilator in the hospital and heavily sedated. I can't get anything out of him."

Zane's phone buzzed just then. He glanced at his screen and made some grunting noises.

"What's going on?" I asked.

"It's a text from my friend Danny."

Also known as Officer Loose Lips. But who was I to complain? He gave us information that no one else would, not even Jackson. *Especially* not Jackson. "What about?"

"I messaged him earlier and asked him if there were any updates on the victim."

"And?" A surge of excitement rushed through me. Anything we could learn would help right now.

"They got the autopsy report back. It turns out Desiree was strangled."

I sucked in a quick breath as I tapped into my internal vat of useless facts. "Strangled? But strangling is usually a crime of passion. It signifies that the killer probably knew the victim."

"Is that right?"

"Yes, it's right. We did a whole episode of *Relentless* on it."

"You have a new theory then?"

The facts spun and spun in my head until I said, "Desiree's boyfriend followed her into town," I told Zane. "On the same day Desiree was killed, her boyfriend was driving and got T-boned. Now he's in the hospital on a ventilator."

"You think he's our guy?"

"I'm thinking he could have followed Desiree here. Maybe she tried to break up with him. Who knows? There was a fight. He could have let his emotions get the best of him—to put it lightly. On his way from the scene, another car could have hit him."

"How do we prove it?" Zane asked.

That was a great question. "I can't talk to him yet —not in his current state. But maybe I can track down Desiree's friend Jennifer."

"Sounds like a plan."

"In the meantime, I have a favor to ask of you."

"Shoot. What is it?"

And then I presented him with my idea.

I'd dropped Zane off at his car so he could get to a massage appointment. When I'd gone inside my place, Sam had been leaving to go to the gym—he'd gotten a week-long pass, apparently.

And I welcomed the free time. If nothing else, I needed to process. I couldn't stand the thought of staying inside—not with Desiree haunting the place —so I planned on grabbing some water and going to the deck.

Before taking a total mental break, I tried to call Jennifer and ask some follow-up questions about Michael Mills. She hadn't answered. In fact, the phone had gone straight to voicemail. I guess I was going to have to wait on those answers.

That was okay. I had plenty of other things to think about. This case. Jackson. My future.

None of those things seemed very hopeful right now, however. And that thought caused a weight to press on my chest.

Before I went outside, I did a quick Internet search for Desiree. I saw all her headshots. I read about her hopefulness in making it big. I studied the pictures of her with her boyfriend, Michael.

I didn't learn anything new. But I did feel like I knew a little more about Desiree.

As I put my computer away, I paused by my father's Bible. It was one of my most treasured possessions—and it had been one of the first things I'd grabbed when I'd packed to move here. I squeezed it to my chest.

Every time I did that—even though it sounded crazy—I felt like I was getting a hug from my dad. His words of wisdom were scribbled inside these pages.

"I could use some of that wisdom now," I muttered. "A lot of it. I wish you were here."

I thought about him. Prayed he was doing okay wherever he might be. Prayed that my mom and her people had decided to leave us alone.

My life was so messed up.

As my phone rang, I saw it was my friend Starla McKnight. She was still out in LA, and I hadn't talked to her in at least a month. I quickly answered.

"Hey, girl!"

"Joey! It's so good to hear your voice. How are you?"

I gave her a quick update on my life, and she gave me a quick update on hers. And then she got to the point of why she'd really called. "Did you hear about Dan and Quincy?"

"No, are they okay?"

"You know how Dan was filming out in Hawaii and Quincy got that role and was filming in New Zealand?"

"I think I did hear that. Why? Did something happen?"

"They split."

My mouth dropped open. "What? No. They're one of the most solid couples I know."

"That's what I thought too. Joey, I'm just not sure anyone's marriage can make it in this business."

My heart pounded in my ears. "You don't?"

"I mean, if your marriage makes it five years, you're practically a superstar. Anyway, I just knew you'd want to hear. I couldn't believe it either . . ."

I'd just prayed that my dad would somehow give me wisdom.

Was that phone call from Starla my answer?

———

After my chat with Starla, I finally did make it to the deck. And my thoughts spun with what she'd shared.

Her words seemed to confirm my fears that relationships and Hollywood couldn't go hand in hand.

I desperately wanted to be wrong.

And I desperately wanted to be with Jackson.

Was I a fool to think I could have the best of both worlds? To think that I was stronger than that?

Past history would tell me yes.

As footfalls sounded nearby, I turned to see . . . Jackson standing there.

My heart raced, first with anticipation over seeing him, and next with trepidation over what bad things might come from this conversation. I didn't want a replay of our earlier argument. Nor did I want Jackson to tell me that something had changed—that maybe he had changed his mind and realized that life with me would be too complicated. Maybe he didn't want a complicated life. Maybe he wanted a simple life with his dog and fishing and working in this small tourist town.

"Hey." I straightened my shoulders.

"Hey." His voice sounded mellow as he stepped toward me, his hands in his jeans pockets.

He stopped beside me, and awkwardness jostled between us. I *hated* awkwardness.

"Joey, I'm—"

"Jackson, I've been thinking—"

We both stopped and shared a smile.

"You go first," I finally said.

"I'm sorry if I acted like a jerk earlier," he told me. "I love you, and I respect you, Joey. But I've seen too many times what can happen when people put themselves in seemingly innocent situations. It opens the door to temptation. And it's not that I think you'd purposefully—"

"Sam is staying with Zane," I blurted.

Zane had an old-fashioned RV that he parked at another friend's house. The side opened up like a tent, and he could "feel the ocean breeze all night," as he liked to talk about.

It would definitely give Sam a true Outer Banks experience.

I'd mentioned it to Zane first, and he'd been totally on board. To my surprise, Sam had been open to the idea also.

Jackson paused and blinked. "What?"

I nodded and looped a hair behind my ear. "I thought about what you said, and, even if I don't agree with it, I wanted to let you know that your opinion is important to me."

"Thank you." His voice sounded husky with emotion as he reached for me.

"I'm sorry that I was being stubborn earlier. It's just that with Eric—"

"I know," Jackson said quietly. "I wasn't trying to be controlling."

"I know." I realized moisture was running down my cheeks and quickly wiped the tears with the back of my hand. "I hate fighting with you."

"I hate fighting with you too."

"And we can tell people we're together," I continued. "It's just that what we have is special, and once the media gets ahold of it, it won't feel as special. It will feel like news. I don't want that."

"I understand."

It was my turn to blink this time. "You do?"

"I do. I don't have the same experiences you do with this kind of thing, so I'm going to have to trust your wisdom."

"Oh, Jackson. Thank you." I threw my arms around him in a hug.

He held me close—close enough that I could feel his heart beating. And he didn't let go. And I didn't want him to. I just wanted to know that we would be okay.

"I love you, Joey," he whispered.

"I love you too. And I know I'm going to mess up more." Like a *lot* more. I had a terrible track record.

"So will I."

Jackson hardly ever messed up, and that was just one more reason I needed him in my life. But at least he was humble enough to know that he wasn't entirely perfect. Just almost.

"So maybe we both just need to be patient with each other," I said.

"That sounds like a great plan." Jackson pulled back until we were face-to-face.

And then he kissed me. Kissed me in a way that I wouldn't be forgetting any time soon—and in a way that I hoped to recreate many times in the future.

As I pulled back, I stayed close enough to still feel his breath on my cheek. "Maybe we should just run away together and forget all of this."

Part of me had hoped he would agree. Then we could run off together and forget about our problems. I knew that wasn't a solution we needed for our problems. But it was tempting.

"We can't do that," Jackson said.

My lips pulled down in a frown. "Okay, but don't say I didn't offer."

Jackson stepped back, his warm gaze still on me. "How about if I go fix us some coffee, and we can sit out here for a while. I can bring out some chairs from the dining room, and we can enjoy this view. Sound good?" Jackson asked.

"Sounds better than good. It sounds great."

"I'll be back then." He disappeared inside.

As he did, I walked over to the railing and leaned against it, thankful a thousand times over that our conversation had gone well. That we were back on solid ground. And that Jackson was still in my life.

Before I could revel in the moment too long, something shifted in front of me.

The railing broke away from the rest of the deck.

I fell face-first toward the concrete beneath me.

CHAPTER
SEVENTEEN

"JOEY!" Jackson yelled.

My arms flailed in the air, and I reached for something to catch myself. There was nothing. Only the sky. The hot-Jell-O atmosphere.

And me in the middle of it. Suspended. Yet falling in slow motion like I was in some kind of Looney Tunes show.

Until my hand hit something.

Wood.

A post from the deck.

Somehow, my fingers managed to grab it, and my body jerked to a halt.

My heart stuttered out of control. I was dangling from the deck.

Two stories stretched below me. Two stories. That

would be enough to crush some bones. Hurt my head.

Kill me?

I didn't know. And I didn't want to find out.

Jackson's face appeared above me. "Joey, I've got you."

He reached for my arm with both of his hands. But my grip was slipping.

I knew I should have done more upper body workouts.

"Can you grab onto me?" Jackson asked, determination in his gaze and his cheeks red with exertion.

I didn't want to let go. But my arm ached. My muscles wanted to give up. And death seemed imminent.

I flung my free hand up and grabbed Jackson's arm. Once I had a grip there, I slowly released my other hand and reached for his wrist. I squeezed my eyes shut, halfway expecting to fall.

But I didn't.

Jackson had hold of me. That look of steely determination lined his face.

"We've got this, Joey," he said. I had a feeling he was talking about more than just saving me from a crushing death.

He jerked his arms and lifted me with a heave.

Then, in what seemed like one fluid motion, he

pulled me again and propelled me upward until I landed on top of him on the deck.

We both gasped for air as we lay there. I was still alive. In one piece. Safe.

That had been close. Too close. I never wanted to feel like I was on a Looney Tunes show again.

"Are you okay?" Jackson asked beside me, his arm still around me.

I did a brief mental evaluation. "I think so."

"You're shaking like a leaf."

I was. The shock of adrenaline had taken a toll. "I know. I can't stop."

Jackson held me as we lay there still. It was like neither of us could move. We had to recover from my near death.

Or maybe not death. Maiming? Near disabling?

I wasn't sure how far it could have gone. I was just grateful that it had only been a scare and nothing more.

Finally, Jackson pushed himself up on his hands and let out a breath. He stood and walked over to examine the deck. As he squatted beside the post where the railing had broken, he let out a grunt.

"What kind of sound is that?" I sat up so I could watch him. Not only because he was a lovely sight to see, but because I wanted to read his body language —his estimation of what had happened.

Had the home inspector somehow missed the fact

that the railing wasn't safe? What exactly had just happened?

He studied the wood. The sight of him being so close to the edge of the deck made me dizzy. I finally closed my eyes, traumatized enough for the day.

"It's a grunt that clearly states this wasn't an accident," he muttered.

My breath caught. Certainly I hadn't heard him correctly. "What do you mean?"

"This wood was cut. Someone was hoping an accident would happen here. And, based on the color of the wood, this was recent. The marks are fresh."

I shivered as I let his words sink in. "Someone wanted me to get hurt."

Jackson's gaze connected with mine. "You know what that means, don't you?"

"It means that I've been sticking my nose where I shouldn't."

"Exactly. And you've made someone nervous. I need to call this in. And then we need to talk."

Two hours later, Jackson and I were still on the deck. One of Jackson's colleagues had already come and made a report. Before he'd left, he put yellow tape over the opening—as if that would stop anyone from falling off. Still, until I could get either a contractor over here or see if Jackson had time to fix it himself, something needed to mark the area.

I'd given up on drinking coffee—besides, it was too hot out here. Instead, I downed another bottle of water as I sat in a dining room chair, Jackson seated beside me in a matching one.

"You did all that today?" Jackson said after I recounted the day's details, including visiting Michael Mills, discovering that Wesley was still in town, and trying unsuccessfully to get up with Jennifer again to ask her more questions.

I nodded, feeling rather proud of myself. "I've been busy."

"And you didn't tell me until now?"

I let my head drop to the side as I recounted the reasons why. "Well, I didn't think you were speaking to me, but I was going to tell you as soon as I got the chance, and I did try to call you—you didn't answer."

"Another domestic situation."

"Seems to be in the air." Jackson had told me before that these situations weren't all that unusual for the area. Couples with marital problems only found their issues getting worse instead of better after they were cooped inside with each other all day.

Jackson frowned. "Unfortunately. Anyway, you're telling me Wesley is in town. His painting is missing.

And Desiree was found in the room where the painting was hidden, correct?"

I nodded. "That sounds right."

"The boyfriend followed Desiree here, and two nights ago got into a car accident. He's on a ventilator and unable to speak."

"Also correct."

"And her friend Jennifer, who also followed her here, is incommunicado?"

"Sounds about right." Desiree certainly had a lot of people following her. Maybe she did have the chops to be an actress.

Jackson shook his head and let out a light chuckle. "You really know how to stir things up."

"I don't mean to. I just followed the evidence. I'm sure you've been doing the same. Except our paths haven't crossed. Which is a little strange." I took a long sip from my sweaty water bottle.

Jackson shifted beside me, and his smile disappeared. "Desiree was strangled, Joey."

I tried not to show that I knew that fact, even though I did. I didn't want to throw Loose Lips under the bus. "Doesn't that usually indicate that it was a crime of passion?"

"It certainly makes her boyfriend look guilty. I talked to his parents—"

"Wait, you knew about Michael?"

"Of course. What kind of detective do you think I am?"

"How did you know about him?"

"I looked at the accident reports from this week and saw that someone from Georgia was in an accident. I followed up to see if there was a connection."

"Brilliant."

"Not really. It's just police work. Anyway, Michael Mills' parents seem to think everything was rosy between their son and Desiree."

I frowned. "When things are rosy between couples, one doesn't follow the other to a different location."

Take me, for example. I'd driven past the police station earlier when I was thinking about Jackson and he hadn't answered my calls. Why had I done that? Because things weren't rosy between Jackson and me.

I really, really needed to rethink my strategy or I might be the one who ended up looking unstable later.

"I'm inclined to agree," Jackson said. "I also tried to call Jennifer to ask her some follow-up questions, but she didn't answer for me either."

"Where did she say she was staying?" I asked. "I mean, I thought everything was booked."

"It is. She told me she managed to find a room at some place that operates similar to Airbnb that had a last-minute cancellation," Jackson said. "I went there, and they said she never checked in."

Another person with a secret. There were a lot of those going around. "She's looking guiltier and guiltier, isn't she?"

"Moving to the top of the suspect list."

"And if Desiree and Michael were having problems, Jennifer would know that."

"I agree," Jackson said. "I need to locate her somehow."

Before I could respond, my phone rang. I saw my agent's name on my phone screen and sucked in a breath. What was she calling about? Because she only called if she had something important to say.

Either way, seeing her name reminded me of just how little time I had left here before I became Joey Hollywood again.

And I wasn't sure I was ready for that.

CHAPTER
EIGHTEEN

"COULD YOU EXCUSE ME FOR A MOMENT?" I asked.

"Of course."

I slipped around the corner, toward the other side of the deck so I could focus—or, better yet, to brace myself for whatever she might say.

"Hi, Tasha. What's going on?"

"I have good news!" Her voice was tinged with excitement. "Fred Compton wants you to star in his next movie!"

The air left my lungs, and I leaned against the house. "Fred Compton does?"

Every movie Fred Compton made was nominated for Oscars and Golden Globes. He was known for making people stars. Not just stars, but serious stars.

The elite of the elite. I was talking George Clooney and Julia Roberts status.

"Are you sure?" I asked.

"I have the offer in writing. He wants you for his next project. It's called *The Invincible*. It's about a tough-as-nails assassin who returns home and finds her biggest challenge is family. It's a wonderful story —a mix of drama and action. I think you'll really love it. Bradley Cooper has already signed on to play the male lead."

"Bradley Cooper?"

"Yes, and they're talking to James Earl Jones about playing one of the other lead roles."

"Wow. I don't know what to say."

"Say yes. What's there to think about?"

A lot. I squeezed my free arm over my chest as my mind raced. "I'm just starting to film *Relentless*."

"And Fred knows that. That's why he's agreed not to start production until six months from now— after *Relentless* is finished filming. He wants you that much."

"I'm . . . I'm flattered. But . . . where is filming? For how long?"

"Fred estimates it will be about six months up in Canada. So you'll still have time to work on *Relentless* if it's picked up for another season. Isn't this great news, Joey?"

My racing heart slowed. "It is, but. . ."

"But what? There shouldn't be any buts here."

"I . . . I just bought a house and . . ." I glanced behind me, thinking of my boyfriend waiting around the corner of the balcony. "It's a long time away. I was just feeling normal."

"Why feel ordinary when you can be extraordinary?"

I was being handed the opportunity of a lifetime. But . . . what would my life look like if I said yes? How would I ever see Jackson? How would our lives meld?

"Joey?" Tasha said.

"I just need to think things through."

"I'm going to send you the script in a few minutes. You only have three days, and Fred needs an answer. But, Joey, you'd be a fool to say no. It would be the biggest mistake you could make, as far as I'm concerned. No one says no to Fred."

Her words caused my heart to race with anxiety. That was a big, bold statement she'd made.

But was she correct?

"Okay, I'll be in touch," I finally said. "Thanks."

When I walked back toward Jackson, I was surprised to see that Adam from next door had wandered over.

I arrived just in time to hear him say, "Wow, what happened?" while staring at the deck.

I observed Adam a moment as he stood there. He wore his bathing suit and no shirt, unashamedly showing off his very defined abs. He looked like he'd just come from the beach, based on the sand still sprinkled across his skin and his sun-kissed face.

"A little accident." Jackson sat up straight, suddenly going into professional mode again.

"I just saw the deck was messed up and thought I'd come over and check on things," Adam continued. His gaze turned toward me and something akin to an apology lingered there. "I know we got started on the wrong foot, and I'm sorry about that. I'm trying to work while away from home, and it's been stressful."

"What do you do?" I asked, curious about the couple and still trying to put together a mental picture of their lives together.

"Commodities trader." Adam shoved his hands into his pocket. "It pays well, but the stress level can get high, if you know what I mean."

"I bet," Jackson said.

Adam glanced at the yellow caution tape before looking back at me and Jackson. "I hope no one was hurt."

I shook my head, remembering dangling from the

boards there, and shuddered. That had been close. Too close.

One never got used to almost losing her life. I could be a case study for that.

"Thankfully, no," Jackson answered.

"I've heard about stuff like this happening when people party on these decks, and the old wood can't hold the weight. Just never thought I'd be anywhere close to witness it. Hopefully, you have some insurance."

"I'll be fine," I said. Insurance was the least of my concerns at the moment. Besides, I couldn't get over the change in Adam's personality. He almost seemed likeable right now. Was it because he hadn't been drinking? Did alcohol make him a different person?

I didn't know. But I did know that people were complex. Most of the people I knew on a deep level weren't all black or all white. Their personalities were a meld of something that met somewhere in the middle.

Kind people could be mean. Mean people could be kind.

Which one defined who a person really was? I didn't know.

He shifted and threw his towel over his other shoulder as he seemed to search for words. "Look, I actually came over for another reason also. I remembered something that I thought might be significant.

You were asking about if I saw anything over here . . . said a crime happened? I've been contemplating whether or not I should share. It might be nothing."

"Please share," Jackson said. "You never know when a detail might lead somewhere."

Adam nodded but still seemed hesitant. "I told you I saw a woman, but I didn't tell you I saw her fighting with a man. I didn't think about this until later, but earlier today I saw some drywall guys working at the house on the other side of me. When I saw their clothes and the splatter there, it triggered a memory. The man she was arguing with had some paint splatter on his jeans. I almost didn't notice it but, when he stepped away, the moonlight hit him."

I exchanged a look with Jackson. I knew what this meant.

It meant that Wesley and Desiree had met.

CHAPTER
NINETEEN

JACKSON POUNDED on Wesley's door as Dizzy and I stood at the base of the stairs. I hadn't told Jackson about the movie offer yet. I needed just the right time, and this wasn't it. Besides, I wanted to chew on things for a while.

I had only three days to decide, and I wasn't sure what I was going to do. I supposed that I would try to help solve this mystery in the meantime. I knew one of the worst things I could do was just sit around and think all day. That would only make me as miserable as Paul Sheldon in *Misery*. I didn't need Kathy Bates to trap me. My thoughts were a prison all of their own at times.

A moment later, the door opened and Wesley stepped out. After Jackson said something undiscernible to him, we all went downstairs to the living room and stood in a tense little circle.

"Wesley . . ." Dizzy muttered, clucking her tongue. "You said I didn't need to do a background check."

"And you believed him?" I asked her. "Never believe people. Criminals aren't going to tell you they're criminals."

I could be so logical when I was dealing with anyone other than myself. It was kind of a shame . . .

"I'm not a criminal!" Wesley threw his hands in the air, a little bit of the Italian—or fake Italian— appearing again.

Seriously, if he started saying Mamma Mia or talking about cannoli, I was going to have to call him out. A last name like Twigg didn't exactly seem authentically Italian.

"A witness placed someone resembling you at the scene talking to Desiree on the night she died. Said the man was arguing with her," Jackson said. "Do you know anything about this?"

Wesley's face paled, which made the smear of red paint across his cheek even more noticeable.

I had to say that between Dizzy's blue eyeshadow and the red paint on his face, the two made quite a landlord/tenant pair.

"I stopped by the house earlier in the evening— probably at 8:30," Wesley said, his words coming faster and faster—and his accent gone again. "Yes. I wanted to get that painting. But then I found that woman sitting there in the dark. I think she was sleeping outside on the porch. I had always heard that there was riffraff in the area who liked to camp out at abandoned houses when they thought no one was there. I just never thought I would see that at my house. I mean, she didn't look like riffraff. She was clean and stuff. I just didn't understand why she was trespassing."

Jackson edged closer. "And what did you do?"

I sucked in a breath, feeling like progress was within reach. If I could figure out who killed Desiree, maybe I could reclaim my house—and my life here, for that matter. At least figuring out this mystery felt tangible. Figuring out my life? Not quite as much.

"I asked her what she was doing there," Wesley said. "She clearly wasn't Joey Darling."

"And she said?" I prodded.

"She had the nerve to ask me what *I* was doing there. Said *I* didn't look like Joey Darling. Then she threatened to call the police, even though it was officially still my house."

"And then?" Jackson had a no-nonsense tone to his voice that I found incredibly attractive—as long as it wasn't directed at me.

Wesley's hands flew in the air as he emphasized every word of his side of the conversation. "I told the woman it was my place and that I needed to go inside. The closing papers hadn't been signed, so I was still within my rights. Then she acted all interested."

"How so?" I asked, unable to stay quiet.

"She asked me if I knew how to find you." Wesley's gaze met mine. "I told her no and that she should go away. The next thing I knew, she was practically attacking me."

"This all happened on the deck?" Jackson squinted, as if he tried to picture the scene playing out.

I tried to picture it also. It couldn't have been pretty.

"That's right. On the deck. I didn't lay a hand on her. I only raised my hands to defend myself. Eventually, I got tired of dealing with her. I had a feeling she'd try to follow me inside my house, and I didn't want that."

"So you left?" Or was this the turning point where everything had gone south and Desiree had ended up dead? I knew that wasn't quite the case. Adam had said he'd seen Wesley leave after their argument. Could he have come back later?

"So I left." Wesley stared at me, as if trying to read if I was accusing him of something. "And that was that. I called Zane and asked him if he'd pick up the painting at closing, which was two days away. Only, as I'm sure you're well aware, when he went to pick it up, he discovered that woman's body in the bedroom where my painting was located."

Wesley closed his eyes. In mourning over Desiree? In mourning over the loss of his painting? The tainting of his house?

Maybe all three.

"So, just to clarify, you have no idea how the woman died?" Jackson stared Wesley down in a manner that would intimidate anyone.

"I have no idea. All I want to do is paint and get paid for my work. I promise. That's the only reason I was there. I didn't want to start trouble. I didn't know the woman was there. And I didn't know she was going to be so determined to get into my house. In fact, she seemed to be rather obsessed with Joey. Desperate, almost."

"Do you have an alibi for later that evening?" Jackson continued.

Wesley's eyes widened. "As a matter of fact, I do. I was here with Dizzy."

My gaze and Jackson's swerved to Dizzy.

She tried to look innocent, but she didn't succeed as she nodded and found her cheap Chinese folded fan. She said she liked to use it for her menopausal moments. But I had a feeling she had more moments of being nosy than she did menopausal lately.

"It's true," Dizzy said. "We drank tea and talked

about things of the non-criminal nature. He's innocent."

"Do you remember what time it was when you drank tea and chatted?" Jackson asked.

"I do," Dizzy said. "My favorite TV show was on —well, my favorite other than *Relentless*. It was ten o'clock."

I frowned. Wesley not only had an alibi, but he had an alibi who was my friend—my aunt, for that matter. Certainly Dizzy wouldn't lie to cover for him, would she? I didn't want to believe it. But she could be a piece of work sometimes. I loved her for it . . . usually.

But, like any smart wannabe detective, I waited until Jackson and I were back in the car before I asked, "What now?"

"I guess it's back to the drawing board." Just as Jackson said the words, his phone rang. When he ended the call, he turned back to me. "That was Billy Corbina from Willie Wahoo's Bar and Grill. We just got a call about disorderly conduct."

"You have to take that one?" I questioned. It seemed like something a beat cop could handle.

"Do I have to? No. Do I want to? Yes."

"Why's that?"

"Because the name of the person they called in about is Jennifer, and she's from Georgia."

Willie Wahoo's was a bar here in town—a bar where less-than-desirable things often happened. Billy Corbina was the owner, and he had his hand in trouble. Yes, trouble. Not specific trouble, just any trouble in the area, it seemed.

However, Willie Wahoo's did have a decent vegan menu, which meant when I was on my vegan kick this was a decent place to get takeout. I was off my vegan kick, and I told myself I was going to eat more protein instead. Or maybe just protein. I couldn't decide.

Figuring out a diet was hard—but not as hard as sticking with one.

We walked into Willie Wahoo's and saw Jennifer standing on top of the bar, singing at the top of her lungs. Half of the patrons there looked amused and the other half perturbed. I wondered if they would like her more if Jennifer sang on key.

Billy met us at the door with a scowl on his face. "She's knocked three people's drinks over. She's got to go."

"Why didn't you get security to get her down?" Jackson asked, his gaze still on Jennifer.

Billy's scowl deepened. "Because it's only four in the afternoon. I don't have security here yet. And every time I try to grab the woman, she runs to the other end of the bar and knocks over another drink. It's a catastrophe in the making."

Jackson nodded slowly and glanced at Billy. "I'll handle this."

This was going to be interesting.

"Jennifer," Jackson called.

She kept dancing and singing "Man, I Feel Like a Woman," acting like she hadn't heard him. She held a spoon in her hand, substituting it for a mic, and her voice cracked with off-key awfulness.

"Jennifer," Jackson said. "You need to get down."

She sang louder.

"Jennifer!"

She paused for long enough to wink and say, "You want to sing with me, Dreamboat?"

I held back a snicker, especially when I saw the tension mounting between Jackson's shoulders. He could manhandle her, but that wouldn't look good, especially since two people had their phones out and directed toward the scene.

"Jennifer, you've got lipstick on your teeth and those pants show your panty line," I called. "This is not the kind of publicity you want."

"Man, I feel like a . . . what?" She froze. Looked down at me. Frowned.

What woman wouldn't take pause at the mention of those things? Who wanted to rise to public awareness on YouTube because they looked like a fool?

Well, some people. But I had a feeling Jennifer wasn't that desperate.

"This isn't the way to be famous," I continued, looking up at her.

Her shoulders sagged. "I just want to have fun."

She was so obviously drunk. Trying to numb her grief? Most likely. But still . . .

"There are better ways," I continued. "Can we talk? About Desiree?"

She stared at me a moment before nodding and starting to come down. But she stumbled on a metal bucket of peanuts.

Jackson lunged forward and caught her before she hit the floor. It really was a Prince Charming type of moment—only it was the wrong woman in Jackson's arms.

"Let's have this conversation in my car," Jackson said, placing Jennifer back on her wobbly feet.

Based on the stares of everyone around us, that was a good idea.

CHAPTER
TWENTY

"WHY HAVE you been lying to us, Jennifer?"
Jackson asked from the front seat of his police cruiser.

I sat beside him, and Jennifer sat in the backseat,
looking rather subdued right now. At least, she was
subdued compared to only five minutes ago when
she'd gone all *Coyote Ugly*.

Jennifer's face paled, but her nose and eyes
remained red. She smelled like alcohol, sweat, and
fried foods.

The woman was going to have a killer headache
after all of this. And probably a boatload of regret. I
only hoped she wouldn't turn to alcohol again to
numb the pain of what alcohol had done the first
time around. It could be such a vicious cycle.

"I didn't mean to lie." Jennifer's eyes pleaded

with both me and Jackson. "I was just . . . I just wasn't telling the whole story."

"Then start talking before I arrest you for impeding an investigation," Jackson said.

Her face went even paler and her nose redder. "Desiree told me she figured out a way to make some extra money and that it wasn't quite scrupulous. But she was desperate. I told her not to do it. That's when I decided to come over here to Nags Head and make sure she behaved."

And the plot thickens . . .

Jackson exchanged a glance with me. "Did she say what she was planning on doing?"

"No, she didn't give me any details. She said the less I knew, the better."

I had an inkling. Was Desiree planning on selling Wesley's prized painting? It made sense to me. The facts all aligned.

"What about her boyfriend, Michael Mills?" Jackson asked. "What was going on between the two of them? Were they in this together?"

Excellent question.

"No, but he's always been a little jealous. He thought Desiree was the most beautiful woman in the world. It was nice, really. Except when it wasn't. I mean, he could be possessive. He didn't like the idea of her being here. He was afraid fame would change her. That she'd be able to get any guy she wanted, and that Desiree would leave him in the dust. So he tried to keep her on a short leash."

"Do you think Michael would hurt her?" The words burned my throat as they left my lips. There had been too many people in relationships hurting each other lately.

"I don't think so. But . . ." Jennifer sighed and shook her head. "I don't know. I'm just a mess over all of this. I should have told Desiree not to come. I should have insisted."

"She was a grown woman," I said. "She made her own choices. All you could do was encourage her to make wise decisions. That's all any of us can do."

"I know, but . . ." Jennifer sighed again. "There was always just something a little vulnerable and desperate about Desiree, you know? She wanted validation, and she wanted it through fame or fortune. She had neither of those things, and that led her to do some unwise things."

"I've seen that a lot," I added. I thought I was beyond that point. I hoped I was. I'd crawled out of the trap I called Hollywood, and now I felt empowered, like I didn't need external affirmation of my worth. I was acting because I wanted to do it not because I needed to.

At least, that's what I'd thought until I'd gotten this movie offer from Fred Compton.

How different would my life look if I took that

job? How would Jackson and I navigate those waters? How would we see each other to grow our relationship?

I'd found a semi-normal life here. I'd found it through new friends. Through Jackson. Through buying a 3,000-square-foot cottage on the ocean.

I pulled my thoughts back to the conversation around me.

"Desiree always thought if only she had this or if she had that . . . then she'd be happy," Jennifer continued. "Then she would have arrived. But nothing was ever good enough. There were always more goals. I don't know . . . I just can't believe she's dead." Jennifer let out another cry.

My heart pounded with compassion. Grief could be a wonderfully terrible thing. Wonderful because it meant you'd loved someone deeply—and that was a gift. But terrible because you'd lost that person and now you only had memories to hold onto.

"Is there anything else you're not telling us, Jennifer?" Jackson asked.

She shook her head. "No."

"Then I'm going to leave you at the station to sober up, and I'll write this off as a warning," Jackson said. "But alcohol isn't the way you want to numb your pain. You'd be wise to keep that in mind. A good counselor can do wonders, and the side effects aren't nearly as embarrassing."

Jennifer nodded, but her bloodshot eyes looked haggard.

Society's cult-like fascination with celebrity and the desire to be famous could be devastating. And Desiree was just one more unfortunate example of just that.

And I prayed that my new relationship with Jackson wouldn't become one more casualty. If it was, I'd have only myself to blame.

"What now?" I asked Jackson as we cruised down the road after leaving Jennifer at the station. Was this the right time to tell him about my phone call with my agent?

I didn't know. But I felt like telling him would only add another layer of stress to our relationship— which had just been restored after our earlier fight. I didn't want to rock the boat again.

But I would have to. Soon.

"Now, you're going to go back to your house and you're going to prove that you can stay there and that ghosts don't exist," Jackson said.

"What? Whoa. Why would I want to do that?" I'd been dreading spending the night at my house all day, and now Jackson was encouraging me to do just that. It wasn't even seven o'clock yet. I had a good two hours of daylight still—even though I was exhausted since I'd met with Phoebe so early this morning and stayed up so late with Sam last night.

"Ghosts aren't real," Jackson reminded me.

"I know. But they feel real. Desiree feels real."

"She was real. But she's not anymore." Jackson continued driving toward my place, and I was powerless to stop him. "It's your house. You paid a lot of money for it. You're going to have to learn to stay there."

He had a point but . . . "Do you have to go back to work?"

"No, I have the rest of the day off." He glanced at me. "I was thinking maybe we could order pizza and try to feel normal."

He would stay with me for a while? And we could try to do something normal? I could handle that. In fact, I craved it.

"That sounds great. Maybe we should get Ripley also." Ripley was Jackson's Australian shepherd. I'd been missing the furry little guy lately.

I had dog-sat him while Jackson was doing his bomb-squad training, and he'd been a faithful—albeit stinky—companion. Sometimes I even thought about dognapping the guy. I mean, not really dognapping, but something close to it—only legal.

"I like the way you think."

Thirty minutes later, we had Ripley and the pizza.

Jackson and I sat on the therapy couch in my living room and chowed down. For a moment, everything did indeed feel normal—and I loved it. That's what I had loved about my life here. I suppose to most people, being mistaken for the detective you played on TV wasn't a bad thing. But for me, everything I had now felt like a slice of ordinary life—and I craved that.

I glanced at Jackson as he rubbed Ripley's face and told him he was a good boy. We sat on the couch, paper plates in the trash, and everything calm around us.

I was going to miss our time together when I left for filming. I could only hope that the old adage about absence making the heart grow fonder was true.

And maybe this was the time I needed to tell Jackson about my earlier phone call. My choice to either take the role or not wouldn't just affect me. It would affect Jackson and our relationship. I didn't know if I liked the possible conclusions as to where that might lead us.

Jackson's life was here, and my life was pulling me away from here. And it wouldn't just be a few weeks. It would end up being almost an entire year.

Then what happened after that? Would *Relentless* get picked up for another season? Would I get more movie offers? How would I balance it all?

I didn't like all the unknowns.

"I need to tell you something," I started, pulling my legs beneath me.

Jackson sat back and turned toward me, his hand brushing my hair and twirling it. "What's that?"

"You know that phone call I got earlier?"

"Yeah, I was wondering if that was something important. We got distracted after your neighbor came over and then with Wesley and Jennifer."

I sucked in a deep breath as I prepared myself to launch into my news. "It was my agent. Fred Compton wants me to be in his next movie."

Jackson's eyebrows shot up. "Fred Compton? He's the guy who did *The Reckoning*, right?"

I nodded. "The one and only."

"That's great, Joey."

I tried to smile. I really did. "I'm honored that he wants me to be in the movie. It would do great things for my career."

"It sounds like it." Jackson tilted his head. "Why do I feel like there's more to this?"

I drew in a shaky breath. This whole dilemma was getting to me more than I'd thought. "It's just that . . . I'll be gone for six months to film *Relentless*. I'd get done with that just in time to leave again and film this movie. It's . . ."

"It sounds like an opportunity you can't pass up," Jackson finished. His voice sounded even-keel, but was there disappointment hidden beneath his nonchalant tone?

Maybe I was reading more into this than I should. Maybe my emotions were clouding my view of how he would react to this. I didn't know.

"You'd think, right?" My throat felt so tight that I could hardly breathe.

"So what's wrong?"

I gazed deeply into the eyes of the man I wanted to build a life with. To have a future with. To be normal with. "It means I would hardly see you."

He nodded slowly, and I couldn't read his expression. "Yes, it does."

Tears poured down my cheeks. I hadn't expected them to come. I didn't exactly consider myself an emotional person, but the weight of the decision was making me feel sick to my stomach. "I don't want that."

Jackson scooted closer and gently wiped the moisture from under my eyes with his thumb. "Joey . . ."

"I feel like I'm on a precipice where I'm having to choose between my career and my personal life. You know that saying about how you can have it all? Well, my dad used to say that you could have it all, just not all of it at the same time."

"Joey, we could work something out. If you

accept the movie role, that doesn't mean I'm going to be out of your life."

Jackson said that now, but I just didn't see how it would all work. Not in reality.

Most men liked having their girlfriends close by. The long-distance thing? It was challenging, even for the most grounded of couples. It wasn't that I thought Jackson wouldn't wait for me. It was just that I worried what would happen during the waiting.

My dad used to always say that relationships were like flowers. They needed to be fed, watered, and nurtured in order to survive. I knew that some of that nurturing could be done through phone conversations and emails and weekend visits.

But was that enough for a truly healthy relationship?

"Listen, you have a lot going on right now, and I know you're stressed," Jackson said. "What did we hear about at church on Sunday? About how we shouldn't worry about tomorrow because tomorrow would worry about itself?"

I nodded. "That sermon could have been custom-designed for me."

"It's a lesson we all need to hear. Let's just take things one day at a time, okay?"

He was right. I was going into major anxiety

mode when I shouldn't. I needed to chill. "One day at a time."

Jackson studied my face for another moment, and I couldn't read his expression. Was he upset by this at all? Or was he taking it in stride?

I had to admit, I thought he'd be a little more upset.

Jackson wiped a hair from my face. "Why don't you let me help you rehearse for your first episode of *Relentless*."

I pulled back my tears, even though my heart still felt heavy. "You'd do that?"

"Of course."

I nodded. Maybe that was just what I needed to distract myself. I needed to sleep on this offer instead of assuming the worst. "Yeah, that sounds great. Thanks."

His voice sounded gentle as he peered at me. "I do need to warn you that I'm not much of an actor."

"I think you'll be fine."

"Does this involve me professing my love?"

"As a matter of fact, it does." I didn't want to leave him, I realized. I didn't consider myself a dependent type of person, but the thought of not seeing him for a month . . . it did something to my heart.

We'd be okay, wouldn't we? We wouldn't

succumb to the same mistakes that other couples made? We were stronger than that.

I grabbed the script from the coffee table and handed it to him. "Let's start on page twenty-three."

He glanced at the paper in his hands. "You'll need to walk me through this."

"Of course. First you're going to need to stand." My throat still burned from unshed tears, but at least Jackson was making the most of this.

He rose to his feet and stood on the living room rug. I stood beside him, and Ripley settled at our feet. The lights around us were on the dim side.

Almost spooky dim.

No, I couldn't think about that now. This was not the time to think about Desiree.

I took Jackson's hand and pulled it to my waist. "You'll need to put your hand here."

Fire rushed through me at Jackson's touch. I hoped that never went away.

"See, isn't this so much better than Sam?" Jackson leaned closer, his voice low and intimate.

"So much better." But my teasing only lasted a moment—because the curtain behind Jackson moved.

Was it an intruder?

Or the ghost of Desiree Williams?

CHAPTER
TWENTY-ONE

I JUMPED into Jackson's arms. But not for long.

He morphed into detective mode and turned, as if expecting to see an intruder.

Instead, the curtain swayed.

He turned toward me, still all bristly and on guard. "What's wrong?"

I pointed, but my voice faltered as I said, "The curtain is moving."

I didn't say out loud what I was thinking, especially the part involving a ghost . . .

Jackson squinted. "That's because the air vent is right below it."

I followed his gaze and saw he was correct. There *was* an air vent there. The AC must have kicked on.

I let out a shaky laugh and tried to compose myself. "Oh, you're right. An air vent."

"I know what you were thinking. It wasn't Desiree's ghost."

"Me? Think that? Never."

"Uh huh."

He stepped closer. "So, where were we? We should stay focused."

"You were about to kiss me." I lifted my head and chided myself for overreacting.

"That's right."

Just as Jackson moved in for a kiss, a noise sounded outside, and I stiffened, trying not to over-react again.

"Is this part of the script?" Jackson asked.

"No, did you hear that?"

"Hear what?"

I froze, waiting to hear it again. All was silent.

"Joey?"

"There was a scratching sound."

Jackson let out a breath and paused. I knew he'd rather be kissing me but . . .

"There it is!" I grabbed his arm as I heard it again.

Something sounded like it was scratching above me. Like maybe Desiree had come from the afterlife and was trying desperately to get to me through the walls.

"Joey, that's a branch scraping the siding."

What? That was too simple, too easy. "How do you know that?"

"Because I know there's a tree on that side of the house. I know what it sounds like. It's nothing to be alarmed about." He kissed my forehead and pulled me into a hug.

"I did almost die today when that railing broke. I'm not all paranoid." I felt foolish, and I didn't like it. I needed to remind him that my actions were justified. In my mind, at least.

"I know. You've had a lot going on. But everything, at the moment, is good." Was I imagining things or was there a slight wistfulness to his voice?

I let out a deep breath. Jackson was right. I just needed to relax.

Jackson shifted and held up the script. "Now about that scene?"

"Right, right. The kissing scene." I wrapped my arms around his neck. "Where were we?"

"I think we were right here." Just as his lips touched mine, a pounding sounded in the distance.

I startled again, nearly jumping out of my skin.

Desiree.

That was definitely Desiree.

I glanced at Jackson. "How can you explain that one, Mr. Smarty Pants?"

Jackson frowned and nodded at something in the distance. "Easy. Someone is at your door."

Michael Mills' father stood on my deck.

It seemed like everyone with an ounce of curiosity could find my place.

Not comforting.

"Can we help you?" Jackson wedged himself in front of me.

Mr. Mills' worried gaze met ours. "I was hoping to talk to Ms. Darling."

I stepped past Jackson, my curiosity kicking into high gear. "Is everything okay?"

He nodded, but he didn't look okay. "It's about my son."

"Come on in and have a seat," I said. "Can I get you something to drink?"

Mr. Mills shook his head as he stepped inside, away from the sticky air of the deck. He didn't move any farther. "No, I'm fine. I don't have much time. My wife is expecting me back at the hospital."

"What's going on?" Jackson's hands went to his hips.

"I'm worried about Michael." Mr. Mills rubbed his hands against his khaki slacks, as if he were anxious. "The doctor took him off the vent, and Michael started talking in his sleep."

"And?" I asked, knowing this was going somewhere but unsure of the destination.

"It was like he was arguing with Desiree. He said, 'Desiree, no. You don't want to do this. Desiree, I love

you. We're meant to be together.' Then he screamed."
Mr. Mills held back a cry.

I drew in a deep breath. "You think your son killed his girlfriend?"

A full-out sob escaped from the man. "I don't know. I don't want to think that my son could be a killer. But he just sounded like he was reliving something, you know?"

It was great that he was coming forward with this, but . . . "Mr. Mills, why are you telling us this? You know that, if you're right, your son could be in serious trouble."

"Desiree was like a daughter to us. And I've always said my son's anger was going to get him in trouble one day. I hope you'll prove me wrong. I hope that this was just a terrible nightmare Michael was having. But I know I can't live with myself if I stay quiet."

"I'll go talk to him," Jackson said. "The doctor was supposed to let me know when he was off the ventilator anyway."

My heart sagged. Jackson was leaving. But I knew why, and I couldn't blame him. But our relationship seemed to be feeding on interruptions, and I'd been so looking forward to just some quiet time with him.

It looked like my career wasn't the only one that would be challenging.

Jackson turned back to me. "You going to be okay here?"

I nodded, pushing aside my earlier dread. "Yeah, of course. You do your thing."

"Okay, I'll leave Ripley to keep you company. Does that work?"

I looked at my alert, blue-eyed, hairy friend. "Perfect."

"Great. I'll call later." He kissed my cheek.

After Jackson and Mr. Mills left, I got ready for bed and lay there, trying not to think about scary things like ghosts or people who'd died in my house.

It was easier said than done. I just needed to talk myself through this.

Okay, so the tree next to the house had brushed its branches against the siding and that could explain one noise.

Then the AC had come on and moved the curtain.

The rattle I'd heard from the room above me? Jackson thought it was probably a shingle rattling on top of the house.

There were explanations for all this.

So why did I keep thinking about Desiree? I reached down and rubbed Ripley's head.

I just needed to distract myself from ghosts and irrational fears and anxiety about potential changes in our relationship. And what better way to distract myself than by thinking about this case?

Wesley had an alibi. I really didn't think he was our guy. But his painting was still missing, and he did need that money. Could he have hired someone?

Michael Mills had a temper, he was possessive, and he'd followed Desiree here. As far as I was concerned, he was still in the running as the bad guy.

Desiree had a side hustle going on. That side hustle possibly involved Wesley's painting.

Jennifer was unstable. But was that just grief? Or was this standard for her? And, if so, did that mean she had something to do with this?

I had no idea. And I had no idea where to look next.

I had nothing. Not really, at least.

But maybe if I got a good night's rest, I'd have some clarity in the morning.

CHAPTER
TWENTY-TWO

MY PHONE JOSTLED me from slumber. I hadn't even realized I'd fallen asleep but apparently, I had. Ripley curled up beside me on the bed.

I rubbed his head.

I was going to miss Ripley also. I was going to miss all of this.

As my phone rang again, I grabbed it, remembering someone was calling and that noise wasn't an alarm clock. I hadn't had my coffee yet, so don't judge.

I glanced at the screen. It was Jackson.

"Morning," I muttered.

"It's nine. And guess what?"

"You found the killer?"

"No. But the doctor cleared me to talk to Michael Mills this morning."

"I thought you went to talk to him last night."

"No, the doctor wouldn't let me into his room. Besides, Michael was still groggy and could hardly speak. I figured it would be okay to wait until this morning. You want to go with me?"

Certainly I hadn't heard him correctly. I sat up and rubbed my eyes to make sure I wasn't dreaming. "You're inviting me along?"

"You're researching for your role, right?"

That was right. The police chief had allowed me to tag along with Jackson before, under the guise of research. It was one of the many ways Jackson and I had bonded early in our relationship.

"I'm absolutely researching for an upcoming episode," I said.

"Do you promise to behave?"

"Of course." I mentally snorted at the no-brainer question.

"You say that every time."

I wanted to be offended, yet I couldn't be. "How do you define behave?"

Jackson chuckled. "I'll pick you up in five."

I ran a hand through my tangled hair and knew my face was going to need some work this morning. "Can you make it ten?"

Thirty minutes later, I'd made myself fairly presentable and Jackson and I were walking toward Michael Mills' room. Our timing was right because his parents were just leaving for breakfast. As we passed them in the hallway, Mr. Mills gave us a soulful look that begged us not to share what he'd told us yesterday. I nodded, trying to reassure him.

As soon as we were in Michael's room, I stood nicely in the background while Jackson stood by his bedside.

It was the first time I'd seen Michael in real life, although I had seen pictures of him online when I'd looked at Desiree's social media accounts. Michael had tattoos all the way down his arms and up his neck. He had messy hair—messy because he was in the hospital? Maybe. But he seemed like the rough-and-tumble type of guy. His eyes were a striking green color, and he had a nice build.

But when Michael's gaze focused on me, our initial conversation got sidetracked.

"Joey Darling? I can't believe you're here. Desiree loved you." Michael's voice sounded raspy, no doubt from the ventilator. He had a small bandage on his forehead, his arm was in a cast, and he probably had other injuries that I couldn't see beneath his gown and blanket.

"Thank you," I told him. "I'm sorry for your loss."

His smile slipped. "Yeah, me too. I still can't believe it. I keep forgetting and expecting her to walk through the door to check on me."

His voice caught, and he looked away, his toughness seeming to melt for a moment.

Michael finally cleared his throat. "Did you ever catch whoever did this? Whoever T-boned me?"

Jackson shook his head. "We found some footage on a nearby camera that gave us the license plates of the vehicle. But, unfortunately, it was stolen. We still don't know who was driving it, but I assure you that we're looking into it."

"Thanks for that update," Michael said.

"Did you find Desiree when you got into town, Michael?" Jackson asked.

He nodded somberly. "I did. I saw her leaving Joey's house and followed her."

"When was this?" Jackson stood by his bed, pen and paper in hand.

"The night she died." Michael's voice cracked as he held back a sob. "I just never thought . . ."

Jackson stayed focused. "You said you followed her?"

I remained quiet against the wall, just like I'd promised. TV shows could convey a lot, but not the gut-wrenching reality of emotions like the ones Michael had to be feeling. The air even felt tight with tension.

"I did follow her," Michael said. "I know I shouldn't have, but I just felt like there were things

Desiree wasn't telling me. I thought I was losing her."

"Let me rewind a bit. You said you found her. Did you talk to Desiree at all after you got into town?"

"I called her on my way here. She told me she'd found a way to earn some more money and that it was really going to help until she could get that role on *Relentless*."

Interesting. That was what Jennifer had told us also.

"Did she say what that way was?" Jackson asked.

"No, she didn't want to say. She said the opportunity fell into her lap."

I still wondered about that painting of Wesley's. Did Desiree discover it was worth one hundred thousand and steal it somehow? We still hadn't located the artwork, so it seemed like a possibility.

I could only assume that Jackson had looked into her finances and that, if Desiree had received a large amount of money, he would know. However, he hadn't mentioned anything to me about it. Not that he was obligated to do that, but it did seem like something he might bring up.

"What happened when you followed her?" Jackson asked.

"She went to a hotel." Michael frowned, his whole face twisting with the action. "I followed her the best I could without being seen. She went to one of the rooms and knocked on the door. A guy answered, and she went inside." His cheeks turned red and it was obvious he was upset.

Okay, I hadn't expected that one.

"And then?" Jackson prodded.

"I waited. I wanted to barge inside and find out what was going on. But I didn't. I figured she might have an explanation. Maybe it was a business transaction. Maybe it was anything but what it looked like." The man's jaw looked like it clenched harder and harder with each new detail that was revealed.

"Keep going."

"But I couldn't stay. Security must have been called on me because I was escorted out. At that point, I was mad. I'd started thinking about worst-case scenarios. I wondered if there was more to this story, and I wanted to talk to Desiree. I kept trying to call her, but she didn't answer."

I held my breath, waiting to see where this story would go. Nowhere good, if I had to guess.

"As I was leaving, I decided to take a drive and cool off a little. Three hours later, I was T-boned."

"What's the name of this hotel? And do you have a room number?" Jackson asked.

"I sure do." Michael recited the information to us.

He was just in time because Michael's doctor came in and announced Michael needed to rest.

But I wasn't totally convinced that Michael wasn't

our guy. He had the rage, the motive, probably the opportunity. But how did we prove it?

———

"What do you think?" I asked Jackson as we walked down the hallway in the hospital.

"I think we need to talk to some people at the hotel and look at some security footage."

"Do you think Michael is guilty?"

Jackson's jaw tightened. He wasn't the kind to throw out theories unless he was fairly confident they were correct. "I have no idea. We don't have very many other leads right now. And the means of death does fit a jealous lover."

I glanced at Jackson, soaking in just how handsome he was. Nothing was as attractive as manly confidence, and Jackson oozed it. "Are you going to the hotel now?"

"Of course. You want to come?"

"I thought you'd never ask."

Five minutes later we pulled up to the Sea Gull Inn. Despite the name, it was a fairly nice establishment located on the oceanfront. I hoped that would work to our advantage. The nicer the place, the more likely they'd have security footage.

Jackson talked to a woman at the front desk, flashed his badge, and then we were directed to the security office. A black man sat at a desk there with multiple screens in front of him. After Jackson explained things, the man pulled up the footage from the day Michael had mentioned.

"Right there." Jackson pointed at the screen. "There's Michael."

We watched as Michael walked down a hallway and paused in front of room 371. He lingered outside the door. Paced. Paced some more—obviously uptight and anxious.

Fast forward an hour, security came and escorted him away.

"Why was he asked to leave the premises?" Jackson asked.

"Someone reported he was making them uncomfortable because he was just lingering in the hallway."

"No idea who did that?"

The guard shook his head. "Just another guest. When we discovered he wasn't staying here, we asked him to leave. He didn't want to, so we had to walk him out. That's not entirely unusual. People try to sneak inside from the beach and use our facilities more often than you'd think."

"Can you rewind to a little earlier? I want to see who went into that room first," Jackson said.

"Of course." The security guard did as Jackson asked.

I sucked in a breath when I saw a living and breathing Desiree there.

She looked so alive with a bright smile and hopeful eyes.

And now that was all over.

In the blink of an eye, Desiree was gone, as were her dreams.

Life could change so quickly.

She knocked at the door. Waited.

A moment later, a man answered. I barely caught sight of his blond hair and thin, short build. But I definitely saw the huge grin that lit his face when he saw her.

She stepped inside his room—but not before the camera caught the man's arms going around her waist.

I couldn't be certain, based on the angle of where Michael was standing, if he would have seen that. The camera was on the wall, closer to the room than Michael was, so he could have just seen Desiree step inside. He may not have seen the embrace she shared with another man.

By all appearances, Desiree was cheating on Michael with this man.

And, if she'd been hanging out so much on my deck, how did she even have time to meet this guy? And what was his name?

It just didn't make sense.

I figured this was about the painting. That was the only thing that had made sense. Until now.

"We need to find out who this guy is," Jackson said.

"I'm sure the clerk at the front desk can help," the guard said.

"Then let's go."

CHAPTER
TWENTY-THREE

JACKSON HAD to go into the station to meet with the chief. Before he'd dropped me off at my place, I had learned that the man at the hotel who'd met with Desiree was named Gordon Haynes. He'd checked out of the Sea Gull Inn yesterday, and the information he'd given the clerk indicated he was from New Jersey.

Jackson and one of his colleagues would try to track him down today.

But right now, as I stood on my deck, I felt desperate to do something else to keep investigative momentum going. Before I could think too hard, Sam called.

"How are you?" I asked. "Making out okay with Zane?"

"Yeah, we're doing just fine. I really like feeling

like I'm a local. We might even try surfing sometime."

"I'm glad it's working out. Thanks for understanding."

"Yeah, I totally get it. I didn't mean to make things awkward for you. That's really the only reason I decided to call. To let you know I'm good. And maybe to set up a time to rehearse later."

"We can do that. But can you give me a day?" Maybe I wouldn't be so preoccupied with this case by then.

"Sure thing. That actually works out better for me too."

"Why's that?"

"Well, I met this girl today."

My eyebrows shot up. "Did you?"

"I know. Isn't that crazy? I just went in to grab some lunch and there she was. Most beautiful woman I've ever seen. I'm going to try and get to know her a little better."

"Best of luck with that."

"Thanks. Wouldn't that be crazy if we both found love here on this island?"

"It would be." Interesting. Maybe the best way for him to get over his heartbreak was by meeting someone to distract him.

Just like I liked to distract myself from my own

problems by focusing on things that were none of my business.

Like Desiree.

Desiree obviously had secrets. What kind of trouble could she have gotten into, though? She was only in town for three days. And how was this Gordon guy connected with what had happened?

Before I could dwell on it too long, arguing from next door floated through the air like a bad stench coming from a bathroom.

Those two could really go at it, couldn't they? The good news was that I hadn't heard Adam pushing Annie around, nor had I heard threats. No, it was just arguing. And the more I listened, the more I realized that Annie seemed to be giving it right back to Adam. While I didn't think they had a healthy marriage, at least I didn't think either was in danger.

But they were certainly a strange couple.

Just then, Adam stormed from the house, slammed the door, and stomped down the stairs.

I knew I shouldn't do it. I shouldn't.

But, despite that, I found myself following him. Maybe it was boredom. Maybe it was curiosity.

I wanted to know what was going on with this family. Where did Adam go every time he stormed away? Was it always to pick up wine and make up?

Since I had nothing better to do, I'd decided to follow him.

Quickly, I climbed into my car, started the igni-
tion, and pulled out behind Adam. I kept a safe
distance behind him as he headed down Beach Road.
Fifteen minutes later, he pulled up to a beachfront
house in the neighboring town of Kill Devil Hills.

Interesting. Not at all what I'd expected him
to do.

The road was packed with tourists, so I couldn't
stop to study what he was doing without causing an
accident. Instead, I found a public parking area, left
my car there, and started toward the sandy sidewalk
that stretched along one side of the road.

I was going to have to play it cool if I didn't want
to be caught here. It wouldn't be hard since it was the
middle of the day and tons of people were out, either
headed to the beach, headed to shop, or headed to
eat at one of the many restaurants in the vicinity.

If I'd had more time, I would have donned a hat
and sunglasses, maybe even a frumpy beach coverup
or something. But instead I had on my favorite jean
shorts and a tank.

My gaze went to a store across the street. It was a
typical tourist trap that sold cheap T-shirts and
boogie boards. But it would be the perfect location
for me to keep an eye on the house and figure out
what Adam was up to.

As soon as traffic cleared, I rushed across the
street. But, instead of stepping inside the shop, I

stopped behind a display of inflatable rafts on the front deck. I pretended to look at them while actually staring at the house Adam had gone to.

The place was charming with white siding and a roof that featured lots of angles. It was one of the newer houses on the street, if I had to guess.

Adam had disappeared inside—I hadn't seen him go to the door, though. I could assume someone else was there because there was a sedan in the driveway.

Just what was he doing here?

"Are you Joey Darling?" someone said beside me. "I'm a huge fan!"

I tried to smile politely at the blonde college-aged girl before quickly turning my gaze back to the house across the street. "I am."

She rambled on about all her favorite episodes of *Relentless*. As she did, I tuned her out. I had no choice.

Because I saw movement in the upstairs window.

I saw Adam standing there.

I saw a woman walk toward him.

Then they kissed.

My mouth dropped open.

What? Adam was cheating on Annie? I knew they had an awful marriage. I also knew they'd been in town for a while. But long enough for all this to develop?

This turn of events had me floored.

"So, what do you say?" the woman beside me asked.

I glanced over at my biggest fan. "What was that?"

"Will you sign me?" She held out her forearm.

"Um . . . of course." I took the pen from her and scrawled my name there. I'd been asked to do weirder things. "It was so nice to meet you."

"You too!" With a slight squeal, she joined her family by the door.

I smiled at them before turning back toward the house. Something strange caught my eye.

Someone wandered the back of the property.

I squinted as I tried to figure out what was going on.

Was that . . . Annie?

It sure looked like it.

She'd followed her husband too, hadn't she? Had she suspected this?

It seemed like a sad way to live out a marriage. A very sad way. And even though my curiosity had been satisfied, I felt anything but satisfied. Maybe I had hoped for a happy ending for the couple. Maybe I'd hoped that between the arguing, they were actually in love.

But I could clearly see that wasn't the case.

This was just one more marriage that was on the rocks.

I watched as Annie snapped a picture on her phone.

She was gathering proof of Adam's affair. Was she planning to leave him? Would she use this as evidence of his indiscretions when or if they went to court?

It made sense to me. But a whole new level of ugliness had been revealed in their relationship.

Before I could leave my covert operation spot behind the rubber rafts, my phone buzzed. I looked down to see a text message from Phoebe.

Can u come to Oh Buoy? Now?

That sounded urgent, so I texted her back that I'd be there in ten.

There was nothing else I could do here—not unless I wanted to insert myself into this marriage. And I didn't. I already knew too much.

Instead, I pulled up to Oh Buoy. Phoebe spotted me from her place behind the counter, muttered something to her manager, and then met me at the front.

"Let's go to my car," she said.

As we climbed into her Jeep, my anxiety grew.

What was so important that she had to speak now and with privacy?

I didn't know, but I already didn't like it. This wasn't like Phoebe. She wasn't the needy or urgent type. Nope, she took everything in stride.

So this had to be serious.

Instead of saying anything, Phoebe pulled out her phone and thrust it into my hands. "Did you see this?"

I took the device from her and gasped when I saw the picture there.

It was a photo of me. With Sam. Our noses practically touched. I wore a PJ set, and we sat on my couch. *The National Instigator* magazine headline read, "Joey Darling and Sam Butler Now an Item."

Man, did this magazine hate me.

Or love me.

It was a fine line when it came to rag mags like this.

"Who could have taken this picture?" I muttered.

Phoebe frowned as she took her phone back. "I have no idea. But a customer in Oh Buoy was talking about it. As soon as I heard, I knew I had to tell you."

My thoughts raced ahead to the implications this image might have. "Has Jackson seen it?"

She shrugged. "I have no idea."

A mental image of the photo fluttered through my

mind. "It looks like Sam and I are dating in this picture, Phoebe."

She frowned again and touched the end of her braided hair. "I know. You two look very happy."

"But we're not!"

She palmed the air. "I know that. Sam must know that. But America might now think otherwise."

I hung my head, feeling an ache forming at my temples. Seriously, why would someone do this? "I can't believe this. It's so intrusive."

"I know you said you and Jackson had a rough week. I wanted to tell you in person—just in case you needed me."

I offered a weak smile at my friend "I appreciate that, Phoebe. I'm going to have to do some damage control."

"Maybe Jackson should hear this from you first." She studied me, waiting for my reaction.

She had a point.

"Yeah, he probably should." I mean, he was a rational man. But with everything that had happened . . . would this test the limits of our relationship? It very well could. "There's more, Phoebe."

She shifted. "What's going on?"

I told her about the movie offer. About how it would take me away for probably a year when I combined it with filming for *Relentless*.

"Sounds like an amazing opportunity," Phoebe said.

"But I'm not sure I can live in both worlds, Phoebe. I'm not sure I can have my cake and eat it too—whatever that means. You know what I'm saying, though, right?"

"That Jackson's life is here and your career will take you away from here?" She said the words softly and with compassion.

I nodded somberly. "Exactly. I don't want to go back to the rat race, but I do want to act."

"I don't know what to say except that I'll pray for wisdom for you." She frowned compassionately. "It sounds like a good problem to have, at least."

I shrugged. "I suppose. Thanks for listening."

"No problem." She let silence fall between us for a minute before changing the subject. "By the way, Sam came in here yesterday."

"Did he?"

"Yes, he was very nice. We chatted for quite a while."

My eyes widened. Sam had told me he'd met someone yesterday. Was he talking about . . . Phoebe? "Did you?"

"Yeah, he came in after working out at the gym. He sat at the bar and we just started talking. He . . . he seemed really great, Joey."

"He's a really nice guy."

Phoebe nodded slowly, almost looking like she wanted to ask more. Instead she said, "I've got to get back in to work. Are you sure you're good?"

Hesitantly, I nodded, even though I felt anything but okay. No, I actually felt like someone was intent on destroying my life. "Yeah, I'm good. I guess I'm going to find out if Jackson really does trust me or not, though."

"Be patient with him. This is new territory for him also. Don't forget that."

I nodded, said goodbye, and climbed back into my own car.

I hadn't taken off yet when my phone buzzed again. Was it Phoebe? Had she forgotten to tell me something? Was more bad news awaiting?

But it wasn't Phoebe.

No, it was something much worse than the picture that had shown up in the online tabloid.

It was a photo of me and Sam. This time we were in bathing suits. On the beach. Lip-locked.

But this photo had never happened. No, someone had altered it.

And if I didn't pay this person ten thousand dollars, it was going public.

CHAPTER
TWENTY-FOUR

WHILE I SAT THERE in the parking lot in my car, I tried to call Jackson.

He didn't answer.

Was he avoiding me? Or was he on a case and unable to answer? Meeting with the chief still?

I had no idea. But my mind went to the worst places. Places where Jackson had seen the photo and somehow thought I was guilty.

All of my insecurities started to rise to the surface. What if Jackson really didn't trust me? What if our relationship was so fragile right now that this was the tipping point? What if this made Jackson realize that being involved with an actress was not the life for him?

My phone rang, and I sucked in a breath. Was it Jackson?

But when I glanced at the screen, Zane's name appeared.

My shoulders slumped along with my hope.

Still, I answered. "Hey, Zane. What's going on?"

"Hey, Joey. Sam and I are at Willie Wahoo's. Want to come and meet us?"

"At Willie Wahoo's?" I repeated. I couldn't think of anything else I'd rather not do.

"I know it's not your favorite place, but I told Sam he had to try their wings."

It sounded like Zane and Sam had bonded. That didn't really surprise me. They were both the life of the party.

I briefly considered my options. Brood alone over what was going on? Or meet with Zane and Sam and distract myself?

Several minutes later, I was sitting with Zane and Sam. I decided to skip the wings and I ate some carrot sticks instead. Everything was loud around me —the music on the overhead, the people who talked, even the sound of Zane eating tortilla chips.

And even though there was no smoking inside, somehow it still seemed smoky in here. Maybe one of the cooks had burned something in the kitchen.

"So what's going on?" I asked the two of them.

I was right. The two of them looked like longtime friends. And they apparently even had inside jokes because all Zane had to say was the word "Frogger" and Sam burst into laughter.

Just as the question left my lips, someone walked past and snapped a picture of me and Sam. Tension squeezed my chest.

Great. More evidence of something that wasn't happening.

Sam didn't seem to mind. He smiled, his eyes sparkling, and said something charming to the passerby. Of course.

Did he even know about the photo of us that had been published? I wasn't going to bring it up now.

"I totally think Zane should get a role in our show," Sam said. "He's great."

"He is," I agreed.

"We watched Bob Ross reruns last night," Sam continued. "I forgot how great his show was. So relaxing."

"It is." I knew I was just going through the motions of this conversation. But I couldn't help think about that blackmail threat I'd gotten.

What was I going to do? Should I pay up? Something inside me rebelled against that on principal alone. The photo was clearly altered. But if it went public, would that only cause more tension between me and Jackson?

That was the last thing I wanted.

Speaking of Jackson . . . I glanced at my phone. He still hadn't called me back.

Maybe he had seen that picture, and now he was upset.

As Zane and Sam stared at me, I realized they must have asked me a question. A question I hadn't heard.

I opened my mouth, ready to fess up to my preoccupation.

"Danny called earlier, looking for the scoop," Zane said.

I straightened. "Officer Loose Lips? The scoop on what?"

"He said he overheard Jackson saying he had some big changes he needed to make in his life— changes that were going to be difficult." Zane studied me. "Anything you need to tell me?"

My cheeks flushed. Certainly Jackson wasn't talking about me, was he? About our relationship?

But before I could say anything, a familiar figure walked past.

I straightened. Was that . . .

It was.

It was the man Desiree had met with at the hotel. Gordon Haynes.

He was here at Willie Wahoo's.

Maybe my luck was changing.

"Excuse me," I muttered, standing from the table.

If the guys responded, I didn't hear them. No, I was laser-focused on the man who'd crossed the restaurant.

I'd taken only five steps toward him when someone intercepted me.

Billy Corbina. Billy with his shaved head, gauge earrings, and overall menacing demeanor.

I let out a sigh. "What do you want, Billy?"

"You've been here twice in a week. I thought you'd never set foot in this place again."

"Well, you thought wrong." I crossed my arms and resisted an eye roll. Or maybe I didn't. It was hard to tell sometimes.

"I like the press you bring when you come."

"That's great." I peered around him, trying to find the man. He was still here. At the bar in the distance.

"But I don't want trouble."

I glanced back at him for long enough to scowl. "You live off trouble, Billy."

"My dad's cut me loose. I can't afford to mess up."

I tilted my entire body, trying to watch Gordon. He ordered a drink. That meant he'd be staying for a while.

"Why'd you stop me, Billy?" I asked him. "Is there something I can do for you?"

He wasn't going to let me past until he got what

he wanted—whether that was a favor or a rise in emotion.

"No, I just wanted to say hi."

"Okay then. Hi." I stepped around him, thankful to have that cleared up.

"Joey?"

I mentally growled as I turned around. "Yes, Billy?"

His eyes sparkled with mischief. "I always knew you were a player."

Anger surged through me. "I'm not a player."

He shrugged. "Okay, if you say so. That photo of you and Sam Butler over there seems to indicate something different."

I didn't have time to argue with Billy now. Instead I continued toward Gordon and slipped into the open seat beside him. I didn't waste any time pretending to show up for a made-up reason.

"I have questions for you," I said.

His eyes widened as he looked over at me. "Do I know you?"

Gordon looked as I'd expected—blond hair that was cut short, a smaller build, and a preppy way of dressing. His demeanor made me think he'd come from money, and that he could be cocky. He nursed his beer, looking like he was ready to stay for a while.

"No, but I know who you are. Kind of—"

"Wait. No. I *do* know you. You're that actress."

His voice rose like he was impressed. "Raven Remington."

"Yes, yes. I'm Raven Remington. But that's not why I'm here. I need to know—"

"Man, I love that show. I'm so glad they're bringing it back."

I was never going to get to the heart of this conversation, was I? "Thank you. I really appreciate that. But—"

"Is that Sam Butler over there?" He glanced behind me "I thought I saw him earlier—"

"Look, that's not why I came over. I have important questions." It was my turn to interrupt now.

His eyes widened again. "For me?"

"For you. It's about Desiree Williams"

"Who is Desiree Williams?" He looked confused with a knot between his eyebrows.

Now this was just annoying. "You know good and well who Desiree Williams is."

He shook his head. "You're wrong. I have no idea who she is."

I sucked in a long, deep breath in order to keep my composure. "We have it on security footage that you were with her. You're from Jersey. You're staying at the Sea Gull Inn. And Desiree met you there on Monday night."

His shoulders slumped. "Oh. You mean Danielle."

So Desiree had used an alias. Why would she do that?

"Okay, Danielle. I need to know what happened between the two of you."

He started to stand, shaking his head back and forth with obvious irritation claiming his features. "I'm done with this conversation."

Oh, no. He was my one lead. I couldn't lose him this easily.

CHAPTER TWENTY-FIVE

I GRABBED GORDON'S ARM. "Wait, this is important."

His nostrils flared as he turned to me. "She ruined my life. I don't want to talk about her anymore."

"Ruined your life enough for you to kill her?"

He froze and his face went slack. "What did you say?"

"Desiree—or Danielle, as you call her—is dead. Murdered."

He let out a long breath and dropped back into his seat, his irritation replaced with stunned disbelief. "What happened?"

"She was strangled."

He let out another breath. "I had no idea."

"You're a suspect, you know. The police are looking for you."

He hung his head, and I almost—almost—felt sorry for him.

"I thought she was done ruining my life."

Now that was an interesting comment to make.

"Can you please walk me through what happened? Maybe I'll put in a good word for you. I have connections in the police department." My connections wouldn't really care but . . . I would try.

"It's not what you think," Gordon insisted.

"Then change my mind."

He raised his head, licked his lips, and glanced at me. "I met Danielle. Is it okay if I call her that?"

"Sure." I didn't care what he called her as long as he shared what happened with me.

"Okay, so I met Danielle on the beach. She was awesome. So sweet and very flirty. We really connected—or so I thought."

"What happened then?"

"The problem is that my wife and I had a fight."

My throat clenched as the picture became clearer in my mind. "I see."

He frowned and stared into his beer, as if tea leaves might magically appear and give him insight into his future. "Actually, my wife and I have been fighting for a while. We came here on vacation, but we're essentially doing our own things. My wife is spending time shopping and at the spa. I've been going to the beach and surfing."

"And Danielle comes into the picture how?"

"I met Danielle during a moment of weakness, I suppose. Like I said, I'm in a low point in my marriage. Danielle and I happened to set up on the beach beside each other, and she was great. We spent the day together. Ate together. I told myself we were just being friendly. She was having relationship troubles also. We could relate."

"Okay." Michael hadn't mentioned anything about relationship troubles, but that was good to know.

"So one thing led to another—and quickly—and we agreed to meet at the hotel that night." His neck seemed to tighten at the words.

I didn't like the picture that was coming together in my mind. "I'm taking it things didn't go well when you met with her."

"That's the problem. Things went great. I mean, I felt horrible afterward. Yet happy. It was confusing. I didn't know what I was going to do. Pursue Danielle? Break things off and beg for my wife's forgiveness? Pray neither woman found out about the other? But it didn't matter because, the next morning, I got pictures."

"Pictures?" Something tried to connect in my mind, but I fought it. I wasn't sure I wanted to face the truth I could feel coming at me like a freight train.

"Yeah, blackmail pictures. Of me and Danielle.

Said if I didn't pay five thousand that they'd send the photos to my wife."

That sounded a little too familiar, and my interest in his story doubled. "So what did you do?"

Gordon ran a hand over his face, his stress over the situation obvious. "It took some finagling, but I managed to move some funds around, and I got the money. I left cash in a trashcan at the beach, just like this person told me."

"And you left? You didn't see who picked it up?"

"And I left. The note said if I stayed around then the agreement was null and void. I wasn't willing to risk it."

"Did your wife find out?"

Gordon let out a bitter laugh. "No, that's the ironic part. She got mad at me about something unrelated and left. Went back home."

"Man, I'm sorry to hear that." But he was a cheater, which made him a big, fat loser in my book.

"I knew it was coming." Gordon took a sip of his beer.

So his wife had left. His new lover was dead and . . . "Yet you're still here."

He shrugged like it wasn't a big deal. "Yeah, I decided to stay in the rental. We'd paid for a whole week, right? I might as well enjoy it."

"I guess your real name isn't Gordon Haynes." He was too smart to leave his real information.

"No, it's not. And I'm not from Jersey. I'm from DC. My name is Jason."

"Well, Jason from DC. You're alone, and you're five thousand dollars poorer—I guess for no good reason."

"I know. I guess I deserve it, though. I should have never met with Danielle at that hotel. It was a stupid move." He took a long sip of his drink.

I studied his face, trying to figure out if he was playing games with me. I didn't think he was. He seemed sincere in what he'd told me. But, then again, a girl could never be too certain about these things. "You really didn't know she was dead?"

"I had no idea."

"Thanks for sharing." I slid out of my chair.

Since Jackson wasn't answering his phone, I decided to text the information on Jason to him.

But I really needed to talk to him.

Jackson still hadn't called me back, and I didn't want to get all stalker-like by calling him endlessly. I mean, six times was enough, right? Or maybe it was eight. Who was counting?

Instead of trying to track him down, I went back to my place, still thinking everything through.

I stood on my deck. It was my new favorite place,

mostly because it didn't require being inside with Desiree's ghost. Ripley stood beside me, a faithful companion—when he wasn't chasing seagulls, at least.

I didn't linger by my railing this time. No, I doubted I'd do that any time soon. Instead, I sat in an old dining room chair that I'd left outside the day before.

Okay, I needed to think this through.

Desiree's side hustle was having an affair with Jason and then blackmailing him.

Someone else was blackmailing me for having an affair I wasn't having.

Yet Desiree was dead, so it wasn't her. Who was helping her?

Was Jennifer secretly involved? Or how about Michael?

There was something I was missing here. Some type of scheme that preyed on other people's sins. That manipulated them. Or maybe a scheme that preyed on the assumed decisions of other people—like me and Sam in that doctored photo.

It didn't matter.

What did matter was that someone had ended up dead because of this. That meant this was way more than a mere game. This was deadly. Someone was willing to take things to the extreme in order to get what they wanted.

"Joey!" someone called.

I glanced over and saw Annie standing on her deck with tears streaming down her face. My heart lurched with compassion. "Hey, Annie."

I stood and stepped closer, sensing something was wrong.

"You said if I needed anything, you'd help, right?" She used the sleeve of her sweatshirt—it was obviously a comfortable "therapy" shirt because it was hot outside—to wipe her tears as she stood facing me.

"Of course. What do you need?"

"Could we talk?" She sniffled. "I don't have any friends here, and I desperately need a listening ear."

"Sure. I'll be right there."

I put Ripley back inside before crossing the space between our houses and joining Annie on the deck. I lightly touched her arm as I stood beside her, feeling terrible for the woman. This was because she'd seen Adam with that other woman, wasn't it? Maybe she'd only suspected he'd been cheating earlier and now it was confirmed.

"Are you okay?" I asked.

Annie shook her head, her eyes looking empty. "Adam has been cheating on me. I followed him today and saw it with my own eyes."

"Oh, Annie. I'm so sorry." This wasn't the time to confess I'd seen it too.

She stared off in the distance, toward the beach and everyone there who looked so easy-going and carefree. "I knew we had problems. I just never knew how deep they went."

"You obviously suspected something was going on."

"I did. I mean, Adam started as the perfect husband. Now it's morphed into this . . . this . . . disaster. I don't know what to do."

"Has he ever hurt you, Annie?" I almost didn't want to ask the question, but I did. I needed to know just how disastrous this was. "I don't mean emotionally. That's bad enough and shouldn't be discounted. But are you in physical danger with him?"

"No, he's never hit me. He's a jerk, but not that kind of jerk."

That was positive, at least.

"Have you ever tried counseling?" I wasn't the best person to offer advice here. I really wasn't. I had a terrible track record with relationships, and I definitely wasn't a moral authority. But maybe I could talk her through things. Maybe I could use my experience for good, somehow.

"No, Adam hasn't been open to it, even though I have mentioned it. He thinks it's for people who are weak."

"Maybe you could ask again," I said.

"Maybe." She fanned her face, as if that might dry

her tears. "I feel so foolish talking to you about this. It's just that I have no one else here."

"How long will you be here, Annie?" Most people stayed a week or two. I had the impression Adam and Annie had been here at least a month.

"We'd planned to stay all summer. We thought being here would help our marriage, you know? It got us away from the grind of everyday life, and Adam can do his job from home."

"I'm sorry things haven't worked out well."

She turned toward me, her eyes still bloodshot with tears. "What should I do?"

My mind raced through possible advice I could give her, but I finally settled on, "I can't tell you what to do. Only you can decide that. If you still think there's hope for your marriage, then, by all means, try to restore your relationship. But maybe separating for a while would help both you and Adam to sort things out."

"You know, you're probably right. Maybe we should be away from each other for a while." Annie shook her head and let out a self-conscious laugh. "I can't believe I've been this stupid."

"Plenty of women have been duped by cheating husbands. He's the stupid one for cheating."

"Thank you." She glanced up at me. "You sound like you have experience."

I shrugged. I didn't share about my horrible

marriage with just anyone and all of those details weren't important now. "Yeah, I've been in some pretty low places."

She fanned her face again and, as another sob escaped, it turned into a cough. "Listen, would you mind grabbing me some water? I left some bottles inside on the table."

"Of course not."

I strode toward the door and opened it. As I looked across the room, I spotted a case of water on the dining room table, just like Annie had said.

I stepped inside to grab a bottle for her.

But, before I could, something hit my head.

And everything went black.

CHAPTER
TWENTY-SIX

I PULLED my eyes open and groaned.

What in the world . . .?

Everything flashed back to me.

Talking to Annie.

Going inside.

Feeling something hit my head.

And now this.

I glanced around. Where was *this*? I appeared to be tied to a chair in an old beach house.

But this wasn't Adam and Annie's. No, this was smaller. More outdated.

I tried to move, but it was no use. My arms and legs were bound to an old rickety chair.

Who had done this? Why?

It had to be Adam.

Was he mad because I was talking to his wife?

I shook my head. No, I didn't think that was it. There was something I was missing, and my subconscious seemed to realize it before my conscious did.

I'd have to think about those details later. For now, I needed to try and figure out a way out of this place.

I tugged my arms again until they ached, until my wrists felt raw.

Whoever had tied me up had done a good job. The ropes were tight.

I let out a sigh and glanced around. Maybe there was another way. Because I wouldn't be getting my hands out of these ties without some help.

The kitchen wasn't too far away—maybe eight feet. If I could scoot there, maybe I could somehow grab one of the knives from the butcher block on the counter. Then I could saw my way out of these ropes. It seemed like a decent idea.

With a little effort, I managed to hop in the chair across the carpeted floor.

Nothing sounded around me, so I assumed no one was here. Maybe that meant I had a little time to figure this out. A little time until the culprit returned.

I prayed that was the case, at least.

Was Jackson looking for me? Or was he so upset that he didn't care anymore?

My heart panged at the thought. I hoped that wasn't true, but things had felt rocky lately. And they'd probably only be getting rockier. Maybe Jackson was realizing he should cut his losses now.

My heart panged again. I couldn't think like that.

Finally, I made it into the kitchen. As I stared at the counter, I wondered exactly how I was going to do this. It was considerably higher than my hands, which were bound behind me, were. And even if I stood, the chair still attached, my fingers still weren't high enough to reach that butcher block.

I glanced around. There were drawers. I might be able to reach into them. Maybe there were some steak knives in one.

I had to find out. It beat sitting here and doing nothing.

I still had no idea who had done this or what this person planned on doing with me.

When he or she came back, would it be my final moments?

Was this the person who'd sent me the blackmail picture?

Jason?

Jennifer?

Michael Mills? No, he was still in the hospital. No way could he do this.

But what if his father was working with him? What if that whole my-son-is-guilty thing was a ruse?

No, I didn't think that was it. I was abducted

inside Adam and Annie's home. Adam was the most likely suspect.

And what about Annie? She'd been on the deck when all of this happened. Had Adam grabbed her as well? Had he hurt her?

My head pounded harder. I had no idea.

Instead, I stood. I strained to reach the knob and finally my fingers connected. I jerked the drawer open. Craning my neck, I spotted silverware inside.

But not sharp knives.

With a groan, I shut it and moved on to the next drawer.

Serving utensils. No knives.

This wasn't looking good. There was only one more drawer, but it was near the corner. My chair would make it nearly impossible to reach it.

I stretched my hand upward, trying to do the impossible, but it was no use.

The last drawer wouldn't be opening.

I sighed and glanced around. There had to be something else I could do.

I thought back to all of my episodes of *Relentless*. What would Raven Remington do?

I remembered one show where she'd managed to bust the chair she was tied to. With the chair in pieces, she freed her hands and feet and later escaped.

Did I dare try that?

I glanced at the linoleum floor beneath me and shuddered.

It would be painful. I could break a bone.

But at least I'd be alive. It was worth a try.

I placed my feet on the floor and rose, the chair rising with me.

Trying to gather all my courage, I closed my eyes and lifted a prayer.

I could do this.

I could do whatever was necessary to survive. It was what every strong heroine did.

But before I could enact my plan, the front door opened.

I froze where I was, and adrenaline caused my heart to jerk an extra beat. I couldn't see the door—I could only hear it as I faced the kitchen cabinet.

And I wasn't sure I wanted to look.

"I don't know what you're planning, but I wouldn't. I just wouldn't."

My gaze fell on the person who'd stepped inside.

"Adam," I muttered, placing the chair back on the floor. "You're behind all of this?"

I wasn't entirely surprised.

He jerked someone in beside him and shoved her in front of him.

Annie. Her eyes were wide with fear and her posture was slumped.

"I'm sorry, Joey." Annie's voice shook with each word. "He told me I had to get you inside or he'd kill me."

Adam extended his gun. "And if you don't cooperate, she'll die."

He'd hurt Annie? That took all of this to an entirely different level.

"No one needs to get hurt," I muttered. "I'm sure we can find a solution here."

"I hope we can." Adam shoved Annie until she landed on the couch in a crumpled heap.

"What's your endgame?" I asked, straining my neck so I could see him from my position facing the counter. I quickly tried to formulate a plan using all of my non-training.

He smirked as he walked over. "You wouldn't have to be involved with this at all—except you had to get nosy. You didn't think I saw you following me today?"

I swallowed hard. Maybe I needed to get a different car. Maybe my bright red Miata wasn't the best for tailing people.

"I was just trying to look out for your wife," I said. "You should let her go and start a new life. There's no need for more people to get hurt because of your actions."

He smirked again. "I read the articles about what happened between you and your husband. At least your maid came forward and verified your story, right? Verified that he'd left you for dead. I can't imagine what you went through."

He jerked my chair around. My neck snapped and the pounding in my head became more prominent. When I finally pulled my squinting eyes open, I saw Adam loosely holding his gun toward me, as if it were a toy.

"Where are we?" I asked, my teeth clenched with anger, fear, and pain. My arms hurt. My wrists hurt. Even my ankle had started hurting again.

I would break my thumb, I decided. That's what people did on TV. How hard and painful could it be? Then I could slip my hands from the ropes and escape.

I tugged at my thumb until pain rippled through me.

It wasn't broken. Not even close. How did people do that? Or was it just another Hollywood ploy?

"I rented a second place, just in case I needed a getaway," Adam said.

"A getaway from your wife?" I asked.

He shrugged. "Everyone needs their own space so they can do their own thing."

"Just go and have your flings," I told him. "There's no need to take this too far."

His smirk turned into an all-out smile. "You think you're so smart, don't you? I tried to get you to shut up. I rigged your deck so it would break and keep you quiet. Unfortunately, it didn't work."

There was something I was missing here. This wasn't just about a bad marriage and an affair.

The breath left my lungs as a theory formed in my mind. Could I be right?

I let out a dry laugh.

I felt certain I was.

There was so much more to this, wasn't there? And I'd been blind to it all.

But Adam had killed Desiree.

It all made sense now.

CHAPTER
TWENTY-SEVEN

"YOU KILLED DESIREE, DIDN'T YOU?" I muttered, disgust roiling in my stomach. I was dealing with a man who would destroy as many lives as necessary to get what he wanted.

I glanced behind him at Annie, hoping she might do something to help. Grab a lamp. Try to sneak away.

But she remained curled in a ball, almost comatose.

If we got out of this situation, it would be up to me.

The thought was horrifying—but I couldn't let that hold me back. Someone had to be the hero here —or die trying.

I tried not to think about the dying part.

"Desiree was a little too . . . too . . ." Adam

pressed his lips together in a dramatic, overblown thinking pose. "I can't think of the word. But believe me, she had to go. I didn't want to do it. But she kept pushing, and I knew she would only get in the way."

I thought about the picture of Sam and me. The blackmail demand. I remembered Jason and his situation. "But this isn't just about your relationship with Annie, is it? It goes deeper than that. You're the one who's been blackmailing people."

Adam's gaze lit with impressivication. Yes, I'd made that word up. But it was fitting. And I loved it.

"And here I thought you wouldn't live up to the character everyone keeps mistaking you for," Adam muttered, glowering down at me. "I was wrong."

"I'm assuming you took the photo of Desiree with Jason as well?" The picture continued to grow clearer in my head. Adam's scheme was far-reaching, and I was probably just skimming the surface here. "You put Desiree up to it. You told her it was a quick way of making money and that no one would get hurt—that was a big fat lie. Then you blackmailed Jason and took his money."

"Very smart, Ms. Darling. Go on. Let's hear what else you came up with."

"I'm guessing Desiree started having second thoughts." At least if I died, I would die with answers. Sadly, that brought me a small measure of satisfaction.

"That's right. She felt guilty. Said she loved her boyfriend. One thing led to another, and she became a liability."

"I'm also guessing that you do this all the time." Adam was no amateur at this. His lack of anxiety clearly showed that. He was experienced.

"Maybe."

"How do you find your victims?" I asked.

"You'd be surprised at how easy it is. All you have to do is be a student of people and you can read the misery on them—hotels and the beach are great places to gather information. It only takes me about a day of watching someone before I know if they're good victim material."

"What a talent."

Adam shrugged as he stood in front of me, looking like he didn't have a care in the world. "I think we've talked enough. Let's get down to business. You need to transfer ten thousand dollars into my offshore bank account. If you don't, I'm going to kill you . . . and Annie."

I sucked in a gulp of air and glanced at Annie. She still stared blankly to the distance.

"Why kill your wife?" I asked. "Why don't you leave her out of this?"

His nostrils flared. "Because she has some lessons to learn also. I told her to mind her own business, but she didn't obey."

Adam must know that his wife had seen him with the other woman today. Then again, this probably wasn't the first time he'd cheated.

"Now, about the money . . ." Adam locked his gaze on mine.

"It's going to be a little hard to transfer money since I'm here with my hands tied. Literally."

"Don't worry—I thought that through." Adam shoved his gun in his waistband and grabbed a laptop computer from a bookshelf in the distance. He pulled up a chair and sat down in front of me. "Give me your password."

"What?"

"Give me the name of your bank and your password. I can do the rest."

If I gave him that information, he'd see what was in my bank account. He'd transfer all of it. And I'd be broke again. Financially ruined. I'd have nothing to fall back on.

Annie living was more important, of course. I just didn't want Adam to win. To get what he wanted and kill us.

I only wished I could think of a way to get out of this.

But I had nothing.

I was at Adam's mercy. And so was Annie.

I swallowed hard before blurting, "I can't remember my password."

Adam's eyes narrowed. "What do you mean?"

"I mean exactly what I told you. I can't remember my password. It's a chronic problem I have. Ask anyone."

"Then how do you usually check your bank account?" His voice rose with agitation. This hadn't been part of his plan.

"Easy. I have an app on my phone, I put my thumbprint there, and ta-da! I have my information." Didn't he know anything about modern banking?

"I guess it's too bad you don't have your phone right now, isn't it?" He scowled and stared at me, as if I'd planned this mystery.

"I try to make things as easy as possible for the criminals in my life."

"You think you're funny, don't you?"

"People say that's my best quality." *Stop talking, Joey. Stop talking.*

"I'm sure we can think of a way to get around this."

"If I guess the wrong password too many times, my online account will freeze and I won't be able to do anything."

This apparently wasn't the way Adam normally did business. No, he usually asked people to leave cash in garbage cans. He might be experienced, but he was simple-minded.

"Are you stalling for time just to mess with me?" His voice came out as a growl, and he shoved his laptop closed.

"Why would I do that? I'd just be delaying the inevitable. I'm telling the truth." I tugged against the ropes around my wrists. They still didn't budge.

"Maybe you're hoping your knight in shining armor will come rescue you." A malicious grin spread across his face. "Don't worry. I sent the picture to him also."

I sucked in a breath. "You what?"

Adam grinned, looking entirely too satisfied. "I decided to have some fun with Photoshop. And since I have you right now, which is an even better way of getting money, what does it hurt?"

Anger surged up my spine, and I struggled against my binds again. "How can you even live with yourself? All you do is go around ruining people's lives to try to better your own."

"I can live with myself just fine—as long as I've got cash." There wasn't even a hint of regret in his voice.

That realization turned my stomach. "You're despicable."

Adam shrugged, unaffected one second and the next instant in my face. He squeezed my jaw and forced me to look at him. "Now we're going to stop talking, and we're going to get this figured out."

"I already told you. I don't know my password." Pain traveled up my face, but I tried not to give him the satisfaction of knowing that.

"Then we can call the bank. There is a password recovery system."

He let go of me by shoving me back. My heart beat harder as the direness of the situation hit me.

I stared at him. He seriously didn't get it, did he? "You think they're going to let me transfer that amount of money over the phone?"

"I do."

"It will take at least twenty-four hours to go through." That was if he was lucky.

"That's okay. As long as I get it."

That meant Adam wasn't planning on letting me walk away from this. Then again, I already knew that, didn't I? The confirmation wasn't one that I wanted.

I needed to think harder about finding a way out. But my hope was beginning to fade.

"Look, aren't there better ways to earn money?" It was a long shot, but I had nothing except my words.

Adam rushed over toward me and leaned down until our noses practically touched. I shuddered at his close proximity. At the feeling of his uneven breath on my cheek. As I could sense the anger pulsating from him.

"This is the way I've chosen, and stop trying to convince me otherwise. Now, enough talking."

He stormed across the room and grabbed Annie. She snapped from her stupor, and terror filled her face as Adam squeezed her arm.

My breath caught.

This was not how I wanted things to go. No, no, no!

"If you don't figure something out, I'll shoot her," Adam growled. "Don't test me."

TWENTY-EIGHT

"I'LL DO WHATEVER YOU WANT," I finally said, my voice quivering with fear. "Give me the phone. I'll call the bank about my password."

I'd do anything to ensure Annie was safe from her maniac of a husband. Why? Partly because I wished someone had done it for me.

"You think I'm stupid? I'm not handing over a phone to you." Adam shoved Annie back onto the couch.

"How else do you propose we go about this, then?" I really had no other ideas.

He paced a moment before pausing and turning toward me. "You're going to send an email to the bank. And I'm going to watch you."

That wasn't going to work. But I needed to explain it to him in a way that wouldn't set off his temper. "But I'll need to log onto my email account in order to get the new link for my new password."

"And that's a problem?"

"Sure it is. I can't remember my password to sign in online."

He growled again. "I should have figured. You're a piece of work, Joey Darling. You mean to tell me you memorize pages and pages of scripts?"

"Numbers are totally different."

He growled again.

"Look, I'm trying to think of a solution here." Sadly, I wasn't lying. I couldn't remember passwords to save my life.

He shoved the gun into his wife's side, causing Annie to gasp with pain. "You'd better think harder."

Panic surged through me. Why couldn't I have left to begin filming early? Then none of this would have happened. Or if I'd minded my own business.

But it was too late for that now.

I had to think and quickly.

"Okay, what do I need if the bank calls me?" I said, trying to think it through. "I probably need my debit card, at least. Maybe my social."

"And let me guess. You don't have those numbers memorized either."

"No. Who does? Do people memorize those?" For real?

He muttered a few not nice things under his breath.

"You're going to have to go get my purse or my phone if you want this 'transaction' to continue."

Adam muttered something else and paced. Finally, he stuck his gun in his waistband, stormed to Annie, and grabbed her arm. "Come on. I can't leave you out here."

She let out a gasp as he pulled her down the hallway.

"Don't hurt her!" I yelled.

They disappeared out of sight. A door opened. Then slammed.

Then Adam was back, waves of adrenaline still emanating from him. "I'm going to go figure out a way to get your purse. You can just stay here until I get back. Try anything funny, and there will be payback."

"What kind of payback?" How far would Adam take this?

Except maybe I didn't want to know. Because this whole situation might not have the happy ending I desired. In movies, the main character rarely died. In real life? It was a definite possibility.

"You don't want to find out," Adam said. "I'll be back, and then we'll get this taken care of. I'd hate to have to take more drastic measures."

My throat clenched at the thought.

What was I going to do?

I had to start by doing something. Anything. No way would I just sit here and wait to die.

I was going to break this chair, I decided.

But I wasn't going to smash it while I was still attached like Raven had done in that one episode.

No, I had a better plan.

I was going to disassemble it spindle by spindle.

The ropes at my wrists were wrapped around those spindles. If I could get them loose, then maybe I could get Annie and we could escape. I could run for help.

There were a lot of uncertainties, but this was the best I could come up with for the time being.

I twisted my neck, trying to see behind me. One of the spindles was already loose. If I could start with that one . . .

I moved my hand up and down and felt the wood jiggle.

I needed to try to push the wooden pieces apart somehow.

I arched my back and pressed my shoulders into the top of the chair. I hoped that might open up the space between the wood.

I could feel the grooves where the wood pegged

into the slats below. If I just pressed into the back a little more . . .

As I stretched against the chair, it suddenly rocked. Rocked. Rocked.

And then fell to the floor with a crash.

Pain spread through my shoulder.

I paused for just long enough to catch my breath.

Then I wiggled my hands.

They were free! Free!

Okay, if I could just get my feet undone . . .

I wiggled until the legs of the chair slipped from the ropes. That loosened them enough that I could take my binds off.

Thank goodness . . .

Wasting no more time, I rushed down the hallway. The first door I came to had a chair wedged in front of it. I threw it to the side and jerked open the door. Annie rushed toward me, still pale but not quite as stoic looking.

"Is he gone?" Her voice was barely audible.

"Yes, but he'll be back any time now. We've got to move." I grabbed her arm and pulled her toward the door.

Before we reached it, it opened.

And Adam stepped inside, gun in hand. It was almost like he'd known we were coming.

CHAPTER
TWENTY-NINE

ANNIE SQUEEZED my arm and hid behind me, letting out a whimper that sounded child-like.

I got to be the hero here.

The problem was, I wasn't great at being the hero.

"Looks like I got back just in time." Adam shoved his gun toward me. "Get back."

I stared at the Glock and knew I had no choice but to do what he said.

I carefully took a step away from the man, Annie still clutching my arm.

What now? Why couldn't I have just been five minutes faster?

He held up my purse. "Look what I found. It's your lucky day."

Lucky day? He obviously had no idea how

unlucky my life had been lately. "How did you get that?"

Had he broken in? I suppose he'd gotten in to leave Desiree's dead body in my house. It shouldn't be a surprise that he could get in to grab my purse.

"I have my ways."

"Did you steal Wesley's painting also?" Was Adam an art thief on top of being an extortionist?

His eyebrows scrunched together. "A painting? No. Why? Should I?"

"Just wondering." I still stared at his gun, my throat tight as I wondered what it would feel like to feel a bullet break through my skin and muscle.

I didn't want to find out.

He reached into my purse and handed me my phone. "Now, why don't you go ahead and sign into that bank account using your fingerprint? No excuses this time."

I swallowed hard, my arms trembling, as I took the phone from him. I stared at the screen. Was there a way I could secretly send a message to Jackson?

Adam seemed to read my mind. "Don't try anything funny."

As if to drive home his point, Adam grabbed Annie's arm and held the gun to her head.

She let out a cry.

My heart rate surged again. "Okay, okay. I've got this. Let me get signed in, and then you're going to have to tell me your bank account information."

He slid a piece of paper across the counter. "I wrote it down for you right here."

He'd come prepared. Awesome. I nibbled on my bottom lip as my account came up. Moving as quickly as I could, I typed in all the information.

I hesitated for just a moment, my finger lingering over the send button.

"Do it," Adam growled.

Annie whimpered again under his touch.

"Okay, okay." I glanced at the screen and hit the button. "Sent."

I showed him my phone and the confirmation screen there. Just as I thought, it would take twenty-four hours for the transfer to go through.

Adam's face lit with a grin. "Good job, Joey Darling."

"Now you can let her go." I nodded at Annie.

He released her.

And, in an instant, Annie transformed from an abused wife into a confident sidekick. Gone were her slumped shoulders and downcast demeanor. In their place was a smug smile and raised head.

I sucked in a breath. What . . . ?

"Thanks for your cooperation, Joey," she muttered, taking her husband's arm. "You're a real lifesaver."

My mouth dropped opened. "You were in this with him?"

I'd been duped. Totally duped. How could I not have seen this?

"When you're husband and wife, you're partners for life, you know?" Annie's eyes gleamed with satisfaction.

"You were taking blackmail pictures today," I muttered, a clearer picture forming in my mind. I thought I'd had this figured out, but it had gone deeper than I thought. "You're in this whole thing together. You both put other people in compromising positions, document it, and then threaten to show the pictures if they don't pay up. Some kind of commodities trader you are."

Adam shrugged, looking rather proud of himself. "I didn't say what kind of commodities I traded."

Con artists. That's what they were. And now killers as well. How could I have fallen for it?

"You're both sick," I muttered. "Really sick. You need help, not more money."

Annie leered in my face. "Now we have to figure out what to do with you."

"You both lured Desiree into doing this, but she didn't like it. So you strangled her and left the body in my house." I knew I should keep my thoughts silent, but I needed to sort them out.

"We didn't figure someone would find her so

soon," Adam said. "But it was just as well that you moved in."

"You did your research and knew about my past history with my ex. You planned those fights, didn't you? So I would feel sorry for Annie." My gaze went to Annie. How could she have done this? Betrayed another woman like this? It disgusted me.

"Sorry. But you have to tap into a person's biggest fears if you're going to hit them where it hurts." She shrugged, without a care in the world. in fact, she looked rather smug. "All's fair in business."

"This isn't business. It's crime."

"I say enough of this talking." Adam sliced his hand through the air. "We need to clean this up and move on. Annie has a date tonight, and she really needs to be more presentable."

Nausea churned in my stomach as I realized just how committed they were to their plan. Nothing would get in their way. Especially not me. "What are you going to do with me?"

"Whatever it is, it has to seem natural," Adam continued. "Strangling Desiree was natural because her boyfriend would look guilty—or poor little Jason. We knew we'd be the last people the police looked at."

"What's your plan for me?" Tension spread throughout my body.

"We're thinking a crazy fan kidnapped you and will send a ransom note," Annie said.

"That already happened." Or had it? I mean, a crazy fan had rescued me. And he'd helped me find a killer. Had he actually abducted me? There was time to think about that later. "It will be like a rerun of reality. You need something better, more creative."

Adam's smile dimmed. "It just so happens that we have other ideas. Like maybe the stress of everything has gotten to you so you just disappear. Maybe you can leave a video diary entry for the world to see. Of course, Annie and I will be on the other side of the camera, holding a gun to your head."

"Honey, we've got to go." Annie glanced at her watch. "I only have an hour, and I've got to get dolled up."

"Of course. You don't want to be late, honey." Adam turned back toward me. "But . . ."

They obviously didn't have time to enact their evil little plan right now.

Maybe that would buy me some time.

Or maybe it would simply draw all of this out.

Buy me time. I had to stick with the idea that this delay would buy me time and try to stay positive here.

"Down the hallway," Adam ordered. "We'll be back later."

I sat with my knees pulled to my chest in a small room filled with a washer, dryer, air handler, and various shelves. The chair must have been propped against the door again because I couldn't open it. Nor could I stop sneezing. Nor could I figure out any other way to escape.

I'd tried. And now I just needed to sit and think.

This was not going to be the end of me. I was going to get out of this. Someway. I just couldn't figure out how yet, but I would. I just needed time.

Unfortunately, between my panicked thoughts on escaping, other pressing life questions haunted me.

Was what Adam and Annie had said true? Had they sent that picture to Jackson? Was he now questioning my loyalty again?

My heart panged at the thought.

I didn't want to believe it. I wanted to believe that I had a happily ever after out there. But maybe they didn't really exist. Maybe not being with Jackson would be the best for both of us.

But if that was true, why did my heart hurt so much at the thought?

I sounded liked a broken record—even to myself —but I had a tendency to mess things up. Yet, for a while, everything between Jackson and me had felt so hopeful.

I had so many decisions to make. Did I accept the role in the new movie? Did I turn it down? And, if I did turn it down, would I resent Jackson?

My head pounded harder. I had no idea, and none of that would matter if I didn't get out of here.

Okay, think, Joey. There's got to be a way to escape.

I glanced around. Most of the things in here, I couldn't use. A washing machine and dryer did me no good, nor did a broom and dustpan.

But . . .

My breath caught. There was an episode of *Relentless* . . .

I straightened as hope surged through me. That was right. Something similar to this happened in one of my episodes. Someone had been trapped when a chair was propped against a door.

I just needed to find something thin and long.

I stood, brushed the dust from my jean shorts, and looked through the shelves where some over-flow kitchen items were stored. Crock pots. A blender —with no blade. Some pots and pans.

Finally, I found what I was looking for.

An old cutting board. It was plastic and thin yet still stiff enough it might work.

It was worth a shot.

I grabbed the lime-green mat and shoved it beneath the door.

It fit!

Victory.

I'd take whatever I could get.

I stretched on my belly in order to try and see beneath the crack. It was nearly impossible . . . but I wasn't giving up. This board was my only hope right now.

I jammed the board until it hit something.

A chair leg.

My heart rate surged.

Maybe—just maybe—this would work.

I continued to thrust the cutting board beneath the door and into the chair leg.

Over and over.

Until the chair finally moved—just a smidgen. But it had moved. *Moved*!

My breath caught.

I could do this. My plan would work. It had to.

I kept working, moving the chair little by little, until finally I heard a crash.

The chair had fallen.

I jumped to my feet and grabbed the door handle. This time, when I pushed, it opened.

I couldn't believe it.

And now I had to move.

But, before I could, I spotted a shadow in the distance.

I braced myself for another fight.

CHAPTER
THIRTY

I GRABBED the cutting board from the floor and held it like a baseball bat—kind of. I mean, as much as I could with a cutting board. And then I braced myself for a faceoff with Adam or Annie.

Instead . . . Jackson stepped from around the corner with his gun drawn.

I gasped and lowered the board. "Jackson?"

"Joey? You're okay." He rushed toward me, not bothering to hide the fact he was studying me for injuries. And then he stopped at my arms and frowned. "You were going to defend yourself with a plastic cutting board?"

I barely heard him. Instead, I dropped the board and threw my arms around his neck. "You came for me."

Jackson drew me close and held me so tightly that I could hardly breathe. "Of course I came for you."

I had no idea how he'd found me. But I'd have to figure that out later. The important thing was that he was here—and Adam and Annie were not.

"I don't have time to ask you a lot of questions now. We've got to get out of here before they come back." I took his arm.

We'd only taken a step when we heard voices outside.

I gripped Jackson's arms. "It's too late."

Jackson glanced around before springing into action. He tossed the cutting board into the bedroom behind us, closed the door to the laundry room, and propped the chair against it.

"What are you doing?" I asked, still holding onto his arm.

"You'll see."

Just as a shadow appeared at the door, he pulled me into the bedroom across the hall. He pressed me into the wall and out of sight before putting a finger over his lips and motioning for me to be quiet.

They were inside, I realized. Adam and Annie. I could hear them talking, though I couldn't make out the words.

Fear ricocheted up my spine. What if they killed both of us?

No, I couldn't think like that. Jackson knew what he was doing.

Their voices came closer. The louder they became, the more my back muscles tensed.

I glanced at Jackson. He stood with his gun drawn right by the door.

I prayed this would work.

Just when the voices were outside our door, Jackson burst from the room, catching them by surprise.

Someone yelled.

Grunted.

Something—or someone—slammed into the wall.

I couldn't just stand here.

I grabbed the lamp from beside me—a much better choice than my earlier cutting board—and stepped into the hallway. Jackson and Adam wrestled for a gun. As Annie lunged toward them to help, I swung the makeshift weapon at her and connected with the side of her head.

She let out a gasp and fell against the wall.

"Sorry," I muttered. "Kind of."

Man, I hoped I hadn't done any permanent damage. But no way would I let her hurt Jackson.

As Adam grabbed the gun from Jackson, I knew I had to do something. Things couldn't end like this.

I charged toward Adam. My head hit his stomach, and he flew backward.

But his gun.

His gun was still in his hand. His hand was beside my abdomen. All it would take was . . . one muscle reaction and I'd be a goner.

Baloney, I remembered.

It was the move my father had taught me. *Below knee.*

Using all my strength, I kicked Adam in the shin.

He let out a gasp and doubled over.

"Put the weapon down," Jackson ordered, wiping blood from his lip with one hand and holding his gun with the other.

As police flooded in behind us, Adam groaned and seemed to realize he was outnumbered. He did as Jackson had told him. While the cops handcuffed Adam and Annie, the pair muttered curses at me.

We were safe, I realized.

We were really safe.

Jackson pulled me away from the craziness and into a corner. His gaze studied me.

"They hurt you . . ." He gently touched my cheek.

Had a bruise already formed there?

"I'll be okay," I told him. As I said the words, I rolled my shoulder and felt another ache there.

This wouldn't be great for filming. But I was so grateful to be alive that I didn't even care. Things could have ended much worse. Much, much worse.

"Jackson?" I said, gazing up at him.

"Yes?"

"Remember earlier when I said I was an excellent judge of people because I was an actress?"

"I do remember that."

I frowned. "Well, I was wrong. Really wrong."

Three hours later, Jackson and I were back at my house. On the deck.

The sun set in the distance. Ripley sat beside us. A pleasant breeze swept through the air. And this whole nightmare was finally over.

Thank goodness.

Instead of going inside, I wrapped my arms around Jackson. He squeezed me back, equally as tight. We were both still trying to comprehend everything that had just happened. It would take a while.

"You're okay," he whispered into my hair. "I was so worried."

"They told me you hated me." The words caused my throat to ache.

"Why would I hate you?"

Did I really need to remind him? "Because of that photo. It wasn't real—"

"I know that, Joey." He said the words easily, as if he unequivocally believed them.

"How do you know?" I stared up into his eyes, trying to read into his soul.

"Because I know you, of course. You're a lot of things, Joey Darling, but you're not a cheater."

"A lot of things?" I wasn't sure if that was a compliment or not.

"You're funny, entertaining, sweet, caring . . . nosy, dramatic, a trouble magnet. But you're not a cheater."

"But you didn't answer my calls and—"

He squeezed my arm as if to reassure me. "I was on assignment. I couldn't have my phone with me. It all came up this morning or I would have told you."

"But someone overheard you telling someone that you were about to make a big life change." I clamped my mouth shut. "I wasn't supposed to say that."

His eyebrows flickered up. "I know that Officer Danny says way more than he should."

"You do?"

"Everyone does. And I was talking about my schedule, not breaking up with you."

"What?"

"I'm going to have to turn down the overtime hours if I'm going to see you. And I definitely want to see you. Whenever you're on a break from filming, I'd love to come down to Wilmington and spend time together. That's the big change I need to make, not ending our relationship."

I buried myself in his chest again, feeling delightfully foolish over my wrong assumption. "I'm so glad to hear that."

"And I'm glad I found you."

I stepped back—only enough so I could see his eyes. I had questions for him. Lots of questions. "How did you know what happened? Where I was?"

"Thanks to the lead you texted me, we were able to track down Jason. He told us the same thing he told you. So we started examining that hotel security video footage some more. I thought I recognized one of the hotel guests there. It was Annie, and she had a camera. I realized—"

"She was the one who must have called security on Michael."

"Most likely. Here's the interesting thing. Remember I told you I'd been to two other scenes this week where there was a domestic disturbance?"

"I do."

"Well, both of those couples were victims of Adam and Annie. I looked more closely at the blackmail photos, and I recognized Adam in one of them."

I squeezed his arm. "Good detective work."

"About that same time, we got the prints back from the truck that T-boned Michael. We were able to clear him after we discovered that the prints matched Annie's, whose real name is Annabelle Cleaver. She and Adam are wanted on various charges in three different states."

"Wow. They were really in this deep. I can't believe I let them con me."

"They were good at what they did—they made a nice six figure income by manipulating people."

"Yes, they did." They'd almost gotten my money, but the police were able to stop the transaction before it went through. The money was back in my account.

"Anyway, I went to your house. Saw you weren't there. And when Adam and Annie left, I followed them."

"You're so brilliant. This whole time I thought this had something to do with a painting."

"Wesley found the painting, by the way."

I tilted my head at the unexpected news. "What do you mean?"

"He'd packed it away when he moved and didn't realize it."

My bottom lip dropped open. "How does someone do that?"

"I guess he literally has hundreds of paintings. He didn't remember packing this particular one. All of his things are in storage until he moves up to Norfolk. He just so happened to be looking for something, and he found the painting."

"He seems a little scatterbrained." It actually sounded like something I might do.

"Yes, he does. But he and Dizzy looked pretty happy together when I stopped by her house a little earlier."

"He and Dizzy?" Had I heard Jackson correctly?

"You should see the way they were looking at each other. I think they might have something to tell us soon."

"Wow. That would be . . . crazy." Dizzy just seemed so happy being single, and Wesley seemed so . . . fakely Italian. Actually, maybe they *would* be good for each other.

Jackson rubbed my arm.

I glanced behind me at my front door, realizing I needed to close the door on a certain chapter of my life. "I'd like to go back into my house."

"What about the ghost?" His voice lilted playfully.

"There are no ghosts—of course." I scoffed before winking at him.

Jackson raised his eyebrows. "Of course."

"Besides, even if ghosts were real, Desiree would now have peace because her murder has been solved. That's what they say on TV shows."

"And we both know that life is a lot like TV shows, right?"

I grinned. "Right."

Jackson put his arm around my waist. "Yeah, let's get inside."

I paused first. "Just one more question."

"What's that?"

"Did you use the photos I gave you?"

"What photos?"

"The ones I gave you in case I ever went missing."

A smile cracked his face, and then a chuckle escaped. "You're something else, Joey Darling. And I love you for it."

He kissed my forehead, and I felt as if my whole world was right here—and that Jackson's arms were the only place I wanted to be. Forever.

A car door slammed in the distance. A moment later, Phoebe appeared on my deck, looking breathless and concerned. "Joey. Jackson. I heard what was going on. Some people came into Oh Buoy and said there were police at this rental house, and that Joey Darling had also been spotted there. Are you okay?"

I nodded, grateful to have people to check on me. "We're fine."

She threw her arms around me then Jackson. "I'm so glad. I was worried."

"I was too," someone said behind her.

I looked over and saw Sam had shown up also. My gaze went to Phoebe. Her eyes lit when she saw him—kind of like mine did when I saw Jackson.

"Sam," she muttered.

"Phoebe?" Sam glanced from her to me. "I didn't realize the two of you knew each other."

"Yes, of course I know Phoebe," I said. "She's only one of my favorite people ever."

"She makes a killer smoothie." Sam grinned, his eyes lit with obvious interest.

Phoebe beamed at his attention. "Thanks. It helps when I have appreciative customers."

"You know what else is good?" Sam seemed to totally forget Jackson and I were even there. His attention was totally focused on Phoebe. "Coffee."

"There's a really great coffeeshop just down the road."

"Maybe we should let them talk and go grab a cup. What do you say?"

"I say that's a great idea." She took his arm before briefly turning back toward Jackson and me. "I'm so glad you're both okay.

I grinned back her. "We're great. You two go enjoy a latte or two."

Jackson and I watched them walk away.

Phoebe and Sam . . . I never thought I'd see *that* happening.

"Is she going to get her heart broken?" Jackson asked, still staring after them.

"I sure hope not." In my gut, I didn't think that would happen. I really hoped my gut was right.

"You know, I have a different idea for this evening, one that doesn't require going inside."

"What does it require?"

"It's a surprise."

I raised my eyebrows this time. "A surprise? I'm intrigued."

"I just need to arrange a few things first. Sound like a plan?"

"Sounds like a plan." As he slipped away to make some kind of phone call, I looked down. I saw the words carved on the deck there.

I had no doubt that Desiree had left them.

I will be somebody.

I only wish I could tell her that she already had been someone.

The only thing I could do was to try and convince other people in Desiree's shoes that there was more to life than Hollywood.

Now I had to figure out what that meant for myself.

CHAPTER THIRTY-ONE

"WHERE ARE WE GOING?" I asked as Jackson rowed the boat out farther into the waters of the Pamlico Sound right off of Rodanthe—a small village on Hatteras Island, about a thirty-minute drive from my new house.

"It's a surprise."

I reached back and rubbed Ripley's fur. He sat behind me, his gaze searching the dark waters around us for any birds, fish, or other creatures that might want to "play."

"You're not going to finish enacting Adam and Annie's plan, are you? Get rid of my body. Take my money."

Jackson glanced at me, that knowing look in his eyes. "Do you really think I'm with you for your money?"

The seriousness of his question seemed to halt even the air around us.

"No, I actually don't. I think you'd like me even if I was poor. Maybe you'd like me even more if I was poor."

He slowed his rowing and frowned. "What does that mean? What's going on, Joey?"

I glanced down at my lap, hating to interrupt this beautiful . . . moment, or whatever it was . . . to bring up my fears. Yet I couldn't ignore them.

"I don't want to leave you, Jackson. I'm afraid of what the time of separation will do for our relationship. I already feel disconnected with you after the past few weeks. We've been so busy that we haven't been able to spend a lot of quality time together. I can only imagine what it's going to be like when I'm down in Wilmington—"

"We'll be fine," Jackson's voice was steady and unwavering.

My gaze locked with his. "How can you be so sure?"

"Because I love you and you love me, and, even when times get rocky, we're going to push through them. That's what couples who make it do."

My heart lifted. "So you think we're going to be a couple who makes it?"

"Yes, of course I do. Why would you even ask?"

"Because we've never really fought until this

week, and . . . I don't know." Not being on the same page with him had really shaken me up.

"Just because we fight doesn't mean we're going to break up."

"But isn't that how all rifts begin? With fights?"

"No. We start to worry when we disagree, but we stop caring about the fact that we're at odds with each other. That's where marriages start to fall apart." Jackson rested the oar inside the boat, and we drifted in the serene water. "Joey, we're not going to have a perfect relationship. There's no such thing. We're going to argue. We're going to disagree. We're not always going to see eye to eye. But that's okay. The best marriages are the ones where a couple knows how to disagree."

I felt the moisture in my eyes. I hadn't realized how much of a burden this had been to me. But my fears—relating back to Eric and me—had pressed on me and caused my confidence in my relationship with Jackson to falter.

Jackson's hand brushed my cheek. "I love you."

"But you know what a mess I am."

"I love you because of your messes. You have a good heart—one that seems to get you in trouble. And I want to be there to bail you out."

"And I want to be there to make sure you don't take yourself too seriously."

He smiled. "And I need that in my life as well. We

balance each other out."

I pulled back my emotions and rested my hand on Jackson's knee, needing to feel connected with him. "What are we going to do when I leave for filming?"

He moved his hand to capture mine and squeezed. "We're going to see each other every chance we get. I'll drive down there on my days off—and I'll make sure I get my days off. And certainly they'll give you a break sometimes, right?"

I shrugged. "I hope so."

"And I'll watch your TV show. It will drive me crazy to see you kissing someone else. The tabloids will drive me crazy when they claim you're dating someone else. But it will be okay. I'll get over it. And if I didn't feel even a twinge of jealousy, then something would be wrong, you know?"

I nodded. "Yeah, I do know."

"What about the movie, Joey?" His voice sounded solemn and his throat looked tight. "What did you decide?"

"I don't know." I'd thought about it and thought about it, but still felt wishy-washy.

"Let me reframe the question. What do you want to do? When all the other factors are stripped away. There's no Outer Banks. No long-distance love. No other issues. What would you choose then?"

"I . . . I want to be in the movie."

"Then do it. Don't let me hold you back."

His words washed over me. They were selfless and loving, but . . . it wasn't quite that easy. There were other factors involved here. "But I want you too."

"I'll be here."

I knew he meant the words, but . . . "It's going to test our relationship."

He leaned closer until our gazes locked. "And we'll be okay."

I squeezed his hand, so grateful that Jackson was in my life. "I love you so much, Jackson Sullivan."

"I love you too." Jackson smiled slowly before glancing around. "We're here. This is what I wanted you to see."

I looked at the water and sucked in a breath at what I saw. "It looks like you put glow sticks in the water."

"That's what I wanted you to see. It's bioluminescent."

My eyes widened. "I've heard about this before."

"It's unusual for this area, but it's been spotted several times in the past week. I was hoping it would be our lucky night."

"It's so beautiful." The top of the water glowed with a bluish green sheen. I'd never seen anything like it before. It was . . . magical.

"It's dinoflagellate that has an enzymatic reaction," Jackson said.

"Is that right?" I had to admit that I was impressed. I had no idea that knowledge was in his wheelhouse.

"Just to be clear, I had to look that information up." Jackson shrugged and let out a quick chuckle. "I figured you would ask."

"Thanks so much for doing this for me, Jackson."

"It's worth it to see your eyes light up like that."

"Joey?" Jackson murmured.

"Yes?"

"This isn't the way I wanted to do this. But I don't want to wait any longer."

"For what?"

"For this."

I glanced at his hand and gasped.

He held a diamond ring.

An *engagement* ring.

"Wait . . . what?" I had to make sure I wasn't seeing things or making assumptions that I shouldn't.

Jackson grinned. "Joey, from the moment I met you, I was fascinated. From the time you threw up all over a dead body and ruined my crime scene, I haven't been able to get you out of my mind."

"No sweeter words have ever been muttered." I couldn't resist the quip.

"The more I've gotten to know you, the more I've

wanted to keep getting to know you. I never thought another woman would consume my thoughts. I never thought I would want to love again. But when I met you, all of that changed."

Warmth stung my eyes at his words, and I could hardly breathe. Gone were all the witty comebacks that I normally attempted. I had to hear what he had to say next. I wouldn't be able to breathe until I did.

"Joey, I can't give you much—no nice houses or fancy vacations. But I'll give you my love and devotion—always. Joey Darling, will you marry me?"

The moisture in my eyes washed over and onto my cheeks. "Are you serious?"

Really, that's the first response that comes to mind? Good one, Joey.

"I mean, yes! Yes!"

With a steady motion, Jackson pulled my left arm forward and slid the ring onto my finger. It fit perfectly.

I pulled my hand close to admire the ring. It was beautiful—probably half a carat, princess-cut with white gold and a thin band. The jewelry wasn't anything extravagant—but I hadn't expected or wanted anything extravagant. I'd had that before, and it didn't mean the promise to love and cherish was any more real.

"Oh, Jackson . . . is this why you've been working so much overtime?"

He shrugged, and I knew the answer was yes.

With tears still rimming my eyes, I leaned closer to Jackson, the boat wobbling as I did so. I ran my hand along his jaw. His face. His hairline.

Jackson was the most wonderful man I'd ever met, and I was so thankful to have him in my life. "I love you, Jackson."

"I love you too, Joey."

Our lips met slowly as we savored the moment— and in order not to tip the boat.

"This should be in a movie sometime," I murmured. "It's magical."

As I said the words, I slapped a mosquito from my neck. Okay, so bugs were never shown in movies. And I could live without them in real life as well. If only that were an option . . .

"I'm not worried so much about movies," Jackson murmured. "I want to live out my own story."

A grin spread across my face. "I do too."

~~~

Thank you so much for reading *Gaffe Out Loud*. If you enjoyed this book, please consider leaving a review!

Keep reading for a preview of *Joke and Dagger*.

NOW AVAILABLE

JOKE AND DAGGER: CHAPTER ONE

"Oh, Joey. You look hideous."

I cast a dirty look at Alistair King as I stepped out of the trailer where I'd just had my makeup done. "I'm supposed to look hideous, so I take that as a compliment."

My dad had taught me that life hack. When someone insults you, don't let them know it bothers you and they'll leave you alone.

I paused on the steps, waiting to hear what else Alistair had to say. Because, whether I wanted to or not, I was going to hear it. As director and producer, he was officially my boss for the next two weeks. The good news was that the only people who would see me like this were the cast and crew of A Useless Ending to a Hard-Fought Life.

Otherwise, this location that had been chosen for

filming should keep me isolated from the rest of the world and safely away from the vultures I called the media.

"You don't understand." Alistair turned away from me, as if repulsed. "I didn't expect Mindy to do such a good job. I mean, your startling bad looks are so realistic. You will not age well."

I licked my teeth—my false teeth, which had skillfully been stained brown and yellow. "I don't even know what to say to that."

"Oh, there's nothing you can say. Absolutely nothing." Alistair pressed his lips together, the edges of his mouth pulling back again in repugnance. Finally, he waved to the crew in the distance. "Let's just get on set."

I watched him as he walked away, and I shook my head.

Alistair King had curly dark hair that poofed atop his head. He reminded me somewhat of Prince. Or was it the Artist Formerly Known as Prince? You know, now that I thought about it, maybe he was now the artist formerly known as the Artist Formerly Known as Prince.

I couldn't keep up with these things.

Alistair was the producer and director of the new movie I was filming here in Lantern Beach, North Carolina. The location was secluded—so secluded you had to take two ferries to get here. But it was beautiful, especially this swath of land. The area jutted out into the water, with an old lighthouse sitting on the tip of the weathered landscape.

As I took a step forward, my thighs rubbed together. Well, not my actual thighs. I was wearing a suit that made me look about fifty pounds heavier.

In truthfulness, at times my actual thighs did brush each other. Whenever I noticed, it usually triggered a crash diet.

I hadn't been able to look at myself in the mirror since Mindy finished transforming me into a seventy-five-year-old woman who'd let herself go. I knew, deep down inside, part of me was more vain than I wanted to admit. I didn't know if I could stomach seeing how I would look with all my newly added imperfections. On a good day—without the suit, the makeup, the added wrinkles, and the false teeth—I was my own worst critic.

Alistair had insisted he needed someone self-confident for this new role in his upcoming movie. I must have everyone fooled because self-confident was not the word I would use to describe myself.

I ignored the stares from the crew as I walked from the row of trailers set up on the perimeter of the space. I had my own moderately sized RV. Production also had one, as well as hair and makeup. The rest of the cast and crew had what was called a triple banger or honeywagon. Basically, it was like an RV that had been divided into hotel rooms—one for each actor and a bathroom for everyone else.

I strode across the sand toward the crew in the distance.

Today was the first day of filming for an indie movie about a retired spy who had moved to an isolated island to grow old and die alone. However, the CIA needed her help to track down one of her old informants—at least, until the bitter end. I won't spoil it for you. Not yet, at least.

I was in between shooting new episodes of my hit TV show, Relentless, and my next big blockbuster-type of movie was still three months away from filming. Some people might call that a break and take a vacation. Me? I signed on to do this indie film.

Alistair was the man who'd first taken a chance on me when I was a nobody in Hollywood. He'd called to see if I would play this part in his upcoming movie and had sent me the script. After reading the first few pages, I knew this could be my breakout role.

This movie would never be a commercial success. But it would contain sweeping cinematography, thought-provoking dialogue, and a hopeless ending. In other words, everyone would hate it—everyone except the critics.

Doing a more serious role like this had been on my bucket list for a while now. Then again, so has having a pedicure where fish ate the dead skin off my feet. Not all my bucket list items were good ideas.

I paused near the production crew and breathed in the fresh air. It was October, but it felt like the summer—until the wind blew, at least. But the sun shone brightly overhead, the waves crashed in the distance, and the fresh scent of the ocean promised that it was a good day for a good day.

"Okay, we need the lighthouse in the background." Alistair circled his hand in the air as he called us to order with the dramatic flair he was known for. "The structure plays an integral role in this story. Don't forget that. It symbolizes how ugly things can be beautiful as well as useful in a society that values attractiveness and youth."

No one could forget. Alistair had only repeated it about fifty times. The man was . . . exacting, to put it mildly. His head seemed to have gotten bigger since I'd last worked with him. Maybe it was because he was more experienced.

I took a quick minute to get myself in the zone. My mind fluttered through all the pages of script I'd tried to memorize. Alistair had sent an updated version last night, which hadn't made me happy. But as boss he called the shots, so I'd do what he asked— to an extent, of course. Any self-respecting actor had boundaries.

I took my position on the steps of the lighthouse.

In a moment, I'd burst inside and start my lines. No doubt there was already a camera rolling inside, waiting for my grand entrance.

"Everyone in place!" Alistair yelled, clapping his hands.

People scrambled around me, moving as if they were afraid to poke the bear.

Alistair quieted. Waited three seconds for good measure. And then yelled, "And, action."

I instantly snapped into the mind-set of my character.

Washington George—yes, that was what he claimed was his real name, even though no one believed him—was my costar. The up-and-coming actor was only twenty-one, and he looked like a young Cary Grant. He'd yet to see me like this.

I wondered if on camera was the best time for it to happen. Then again, Alistair liked "organic acting" as he called it.

Fully immersed in the character of Drusilla Fair-weather, I stared up at the lighthouse. Forcing myself to look pensive, I slowly climbed the steps.

I paused at the doorway, my hand on the handle. I took one last glance behind me, as if I feared being followed. I had a lot of real-life experience to tap into for that emotion.

Finally, after a moment of dramatic thought, where I'd actually found myself thinking about the plight of the seagull, I opened the door. I froze. Then I screamed and nearly tumbled backward.

Washington George lay at the base of the stairs.

Dead.

With blood pooling around his head and trickling from his mouth.

Click here to continue reading.

ALSO BY CHRISTY BARRITT:

THE WORST DETECTIVE EVER

I'm not really a private detective. I just play one on TV.

Joey Darling, better known to the world as Raven Remington, detective extraordinaire, is trying to separate herself from her invincible alter ego. She played the spunky character for five years on the hit TV show *Relentless*, which catapulted her to fame and into the role of Hollywood's sweetheart. When her marriage falls apart, her finances dwindle to nothing, and her father disappears, Joey finds herself on the Outer Banks of North Carolina, trying to piece together her life away from the limelight. But as people continually mistake her for the character she played on TV, she's tasked with solving real life crimes . . . even though she's terrible at it.

ABOUT THE AUTHOR

USA Today has called Christy Barritt's books "scary, funny, passionate, and quirky."

Christy writes both mystery and romantic suspense novels that are clean with underlying messages of faith. Her books have sold more than three million copies and have won the Daphne du Maurier Award for Excellence in Suspense and Mystery, have been twice nominated for the Romantic Times Reviewers' Choice Award, and have finaled for both a Carol Award and Foreword Magazine's Book of the Year.

She is married to her Prince Charming, a man who thinks she's hilarious—but only when she's not trying to be. Christy is a self-proclaimed klutz, an avid music lover who's known for spontaneously bursting into song, and a road trip aficionado.

When she's not working or spending time with her family, she enjoys singing, playing the guitar, and exploring small, unsuspecting towns where people have no idea how accident-prone she is.

Find Christy online at:
www.christybarritt.com
www.facebook.com/christybarritt
www.twitter.com/cbarritt

Sign up for Christy's newsletter to get information on all of her latest releases here: **www.christybarritt. com/newsletter-sign-up/**

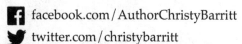
facebook.com/AuthorChristyBarritt
twitter.com/christybarritt
instagram.com/cebarritt

.